Crossed Up

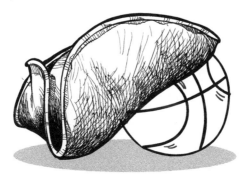

Suite 300 - 990 Fort St
Victoria, BC, V8V 3K2
Canada

www.friesenpress.com

Copyright © 2018 by M L Rosynek
First Edition — 2018

ISBN
978-1-5255-2383-0 (Hardcover)
978-1-5255-2384-7 (Paperback)
978-1-5255-2385-4 (eBook)

1. JUVENILE FICTION, SPORTS & RECREATION, BASKETBALL

Distributed to the trade by The Ingram Book Company

Crossed Up

A Tale of Hitting the Boards and Walking the Plank

M L ROSYNEK

‡ Tip Off

The Beginning, Galveston 1821

Thomas

It's all happening too quickly. We have to hurry if the plan is going to work. I imagine Simone pacing back and forth in her room above the hotel. She's truly beautiful and means the world to me. All I want is to make it through the night and return to her. She seemed so upset when I told her that I had to go through with my plans for tonight before she and I could leave and begin a new life together.

"Why?" she asked. "We don't need to be rich, and we have each other." She started sobbing, and I saw the pain written on her face.

As I started to leave, she fell on her knees while grabbing her dress. I couldn't bear to look back at her for fear I would change my mind. I don't think she understands that if I don't go through with tonight, we may not have a future together. Jean Lafitte would make sure of that. He is not one to be messed with. If you want to escape his grasp, you must have a highly thought-out plan. (The monetary rewards won't hurt though. Our newfound riches will make life much easier.)

Maison Rouge is the home of Jean Lafitte, and it is unusually busy this evening. I keep my head down as I pick up my pace. My destination is the infamous red house, and I will be expected to participate in whatever sordid activity he asks of me. Technically, it is summer on the coast, which means it's humid. This evening, however, is chillier than most, and the skies indicate a big storm is on the way. I just pray the rain will hold off for a bit longer. That is all I need.

I notice people scurrying around gathering their belongings. The main house is surrounded by numerous smaller shacks. The homesteads collectively make up the dictator's village, Campeche. I know these single-room homes are touted as quaint and homey, but in reality, they are plain, barren, and cold. I never understood how Lafitte was able to convince so many people to pursue their fortune here while treating him like a king. It doesn't matter now though. His reign is over. He is being forced to leave. Tonight.

Surprisingly, everyone is still listening to him and helping him. Why? I will never understand the hold he has on this village. It's fascinating. I assume these people were enticed by promises to get them to relocate here. Many nights have been filled with laughter, games, and dreams of economic success. The men work in the trade business and help with the fleet of ships, which kept coming and going. The women raise their children, and the port of Galveston is forever grateful that their city is recognized all over the world. However, all their prosperity has occurred under a not-so-subtle veil of corruption. The ships are now pirate ships, and the man in charge is none other than Jean Lafitte, the most notorious pirate to have ever lived.

Lafitte is a charismatic man, to be sure. Looking back, I can hardly believe that a famous thief is able to schmooze his way into the good graces of governors and royalty. With a wink of an eye and a firm handshake or a reassuring stroke on the arm, Lafitte has a way of making even the most suspicious person become vulnerable. He was a hero back in New Orleans. Despite stealing what he later sold for huge discounts, people were just grateful to have him on their side. He was treated to lavish dinners, and the authorities used to feel it best to turn a blind eye to any illegal misconduct. It was much more important to have the finest rugs, linens, liquor, and jewels in their household than worry about how it had been acquired. Lafitte was basically untouchable. I doubt he would have left Cajun country had it not been for his insatiable appetite for beautiful women. The current object of his affections has raven hair and is elegant in her dress. She is also unobtainable. She is the governor's wife. We have all heard her name over the course of time in this community. If you drink enough during late nights with Lafitte, you will eventually hear her name cross his lips. He has never been the same since. He has turned bitter over the years. Perhaps she is why he was kicked out of his new city. He has turned mean and vengeful. No one is safe anymore.

Wouldn't you know it, it's sprinkling now. I'm betting the storm will soon be upon us. Escaping in uncertain weather will only make things more difficult.

I see the glow emanating from the red house, and I head up its pathway. Few people are allowed into Lafitte's home. I have had access to his great manor ever since I saved some stolen coins from falling to the ocean floor. Money buys friends and special favors. Lafitte loves his money.

The front door is slightly open, and I hear voices inside. I take off my hat, shake the excess water from it, and then hold it by my side. Now is not the time to be nervous. I push the door open all the way.

I hear Lafitte speaking loudly in the vicinity of the parlor. As I make my way toward the double doors, I spot the guests looking down at the wooden floor. Lafitte is pacing back and forth in front of them while detailing his list of demands. "I want the ship packed with all the items. Don't let on to the other crews that their ships are worthless. Pack any person who is leaving onto one of those other two ships, not mine. If they make it, they make it, but I don't care. I want to get out of here before the storm gets worse."

I must have made a small gulping sound, because everyone turns around and notices me. Lafitte gives me a sly welcoming grin. "Good, you're here. The biggest honor is going to be given to you." He strokes his mustache, which is going gray on the ends. "I'm entrusting you, Thomas, to oversee the gold as well as the coins. Nothing matters to me more than protecting them. Can I trust you?"

Lafitte approaches me until he is mere inches from my face. We stare into each other's eyes. I'm fairly tall, but Lafitte is taller. He still has a full head of hair, and he always dresses to impress. His waistcoat touches my hands. I just hope he doesn't feel me shaking.

"You have my word," I say. Lafitte holds my stare a bit longer before he displays a crooked smile. His rests his hand on my shoulder, then turns and walks back to his desk.

It's show time.

The room goes quiet, and we all await the arrival of Evelyne. She is kin to the legendary Marie Leveau. No important event in Lafitte's life has ever occurred without him first seeking the private council of the queen's ancient magic.

She finally arrives with her usual grandeur. The heavyset woman wears a colorful tribal turban in shades of turquoise, which helps offset her smooth dark skin. From this point on, we will do what she tells us to do.

The ritual begins in much the same way as her other spells. The room is dim, and the only noise to be heard is Evelyne humming ever so softly. The tune is difficult to decipher, but knowing Evelyne, it originated from the island of Martinique. Ms. E, as she is known, is a firm believer in gris-gris, which is a mixture of black and white magic. She believes no one is all good or all evil. She insists that she is inspired by her dreams, hence the music she selects to sing or hum. Tonight, I'm not feeling the pitches of her notes, but I dare not say a word. How ironic that her music is believed to help open the gateways between many worlds. I suppose I will soon see if this theory is accurate.

The grand mistress is quickly overcome by her own trance. She sways right and left ever so slightly. Her eyes remain tightly closed, and her hands face the sky. "Zombi, Zombi, Zombi . . .." she chants. Without opening her eyes, she places a large wooden box on the floor as she sings louder.

I peek around to see where everyone else is standing. I notice Lafitte's three favorite slaves are immersed in every word that comes from the lady's mouth. One slave, Caesar, is a midget. I'm sure many would question what this small man can actually do for his employer, but Caesar's small stature has made him even more eager to please. We all know how much Lafitte enjoys attention.

I scoot over to stand alongside the slaves. Before I know it, Mrs. E. guides us into a small circle around the infamous box. I recall having seen some of these details played out once before and realize that tonight Zombie will not make it out alive. The evening's sacrifice is a small black snake, which Evelyne thrusts over her head. She places the unsuspecting serpent inside the wooden cube and turns the lock. In the blink of an eye, the priestess pulls out a shiny sword from her layers of white broadcloth and forces it ever so slowly inside the box. She opens the box and dumps the doomed creature into a waiting pot of boiling liquid. I dare not ask what the liquid is.

She places several small cups in front of us, and I'm guessing we will be expected to drink the recently created mixture. I imagine that I'm drinking a steaming cup of afternoon tea but with an added touch of magic. Maybe I would be better at pretending I'm taking a shot of something stronger. It's probably best that I try not to think at all and just chug it, which I do. There, it's over. The problem is, I have no idea what I just drank or its intended purpose. Unfortunately, the potion leaves a strong aftertaste that resembles grass and undercooked meat.

Suddenly, the room sways before me, and the floor begins to resemble the moving waves from the oceans we travel so frequently. Wow! I see two Caesars. Even worse, there are now two Lafittes in front of me. I try to sit down but fail to maneuver my rear end into the waiting chair. Maybe this is a blessing in disguise, because now I have an excuse to get myself out of this room once and for all.

As I try to regain my composure, earlier events from my memory of the evening seep into my mind. Mostly, I think about Simone. I can't shake the image of her lying on the ground and how helpless she looked. It took everything in me not to turn around, scoop her up, and run off somewhere. I remind myself that I'm risking so much, but it's all for her. For us.

I gather my coat, hat, and my flask and head toward my other lady friend, the awaiting ship. Luckily, the flask is still full from last night. I had anticipated my need for some liquid courage. After ensuring no one can see me, I unscrew the cap and take a big gulp of the dark rum. Immediately, I feel the warmth of the drink entering my limbs. Pirates and rum are a natural fit, but I still hesitate before allowing others to see me drink it. I have hidden a couple of navigational charts inside my boots. I was careful not to get them wet, so I could preserve all the important markings. I don't anticipate going far. In fact, we may all become collateral damage if my plan doesn't work. Lafitte doesn't like any loose ends, and he forms no attachments. I assume the other two ships are stopping near Louisiana as a decoy. The skeleton crew onboard my ship is making final preparations. There is not a lot of time. The inclement weather, coupled with Galveston's law, is forcing them all out at dawn. We will have to make do. The only thing left is Lafitte himself.

His arrogance is legendary. I can only imagine that he is still primping before he makes his way onto his stolen ship one last time. His followers just left without anything but the clothes on their backs and a false promise of splitting the fortune when the ship docks. Lafitte's numerous trunks, stuffed with his finest European frocks, are already on board. His jewelry is real gold, and he even packed his down bedding. It's too bad he won't see any of it again.

I command the crew to go below while I take one final look around. No questions are asked, and the five men hastily retreat. I make no warning sounds or give any indication that something is amiss. With one quick scoop, I shut the large wooden door and secure the heavy exterior locks. The men have no time to suspect anything or react before being trapped inside the secluded cabin.

I scurry back on deck and grab ropes and a buoy. The ship has already begun to move, and luckily, the current is picking up. It doesn't matter, because there was no way Lafitte can reach us. I feel a mixture of sweat and rain on my body. My adrenaline is pumping. No matter how long I may have planned all this, I can't believe it's actually happening.

I dare to look up for a moment, and when I do, I see Lafitte standing on the shore, watching me. I don't know what I was expecting him to do or how I thought he would react, but this wasn't it. He stands there, silent. Our eyes lock again, just as they did in the parlor. I don't know if he is in shock or maybe slightly impressed that I have outmaneuvered him. A slight uneasiness threatens to consume me. I have to block it out.

I turn away as the ship picks up speed. Closing my eyes, I remember Simone's golden-brown hair touching my cheek and the way her eyes turn up at the corners when she laughs. I'm doing this for us. It will all be worth it. Despite the ship sailing off on pitch-black waters, I'm still not convinced that we are out of Lafitte's grasp. I have become familiar with this large schooner. The *Pride* is Lafitte's current obsession, if you will. It is beautiful, as pirate ships go, and filled with the most useful weapons. She was stolen from the Spanish. Lafitte always hated the Spanish. I will never know if his hatred is personal or due to the fact that he has been offered so many lucrative deals to go after them in exchange for safe harbor. Simone is Spanish. I never told Lafitte that.

Lafitte's silhouette is growing increasingly distant. I want to believe we are "smooth sailing" (bad pun intended), but I can't shake the lasting impression of his face staring at me from the darkening shoreline. The most disconcerting thing was seeing him standing there with one eye shut. He only does that when he is contemplating something serious or even sinister.

I look up into the dark of night with only the sounds of the ocean to keep me from going mad. These ships are all known as the "Terror of the Gulf of Mexico," even for those who man them. I feel an urge to strip down the black flag of Cartagena that is flying proudly above me. I want every last trace of that man stripped away. From now on, I have to focus on my future, most importantly, Simone.

Simone

My eyes are swollen and burning. I want to skip ahead to when Thomas and I are together. All I can think about is my future and being with Thomas. Hopefully, we will be somewhere new and have a real home. Life as a chambermaid in a hotel isn't the proper way to raise a child. I'm pregnant. I wanted to tell Thomas. I know he will be thrilled to find out he is going to be a father. I was almost able to get the words out of my mouth, but he changed the course of our conversation. All I remember is him informing me that he had to make one last journey with that man. I'm certain he recognized how upset I was.

"You've turned white," he said. "Simone, it's the last time. Lafitte is being forced to leave. If I don't finish up and help him, he will have me killed. I have a plan. You have to trust me," Thomas pleaded. Every time there's another trip, people don't return. This trip is especially frightening. It is everyone for themselves.

I focus on getting myself back together. I walk toward my small closet and rummage through a few clean dresses. This one. It's pretty and will lift my mood. Despite knowing that Thomas won't see me in it, I imagine his expression, should he magically appear. He would smile and reach for my hand. He would whisper in my ear and tell me how beautiful I am and kiss my cheek. It is this type of stolen moment that keeps me going. I love Thomas. I can't wait to be the mother to his child.

I don't have to work tonight, and I'm grateful for that. Emotionally, I can't handle it right now. I think I will make some hot tea and have a small plate of cheese and meat that I confiscated from the kitchen earlier. Luckily, the head cook is quite generous with leftovers. I will focus on the welcoming plate of food and a new book that one of the guests left behind.

As I sit, I hear a slight tapping on the door. *Please, no. I don't want to be called in,* I think. The tapping continues, and I realize I can't ignore it. I glance in the mirror. I've looked better, but I'm still presentable.

"Who is it?" I ask. I hear a response that sounds so ominous it makes the hairs on my neck stand up.

"Why, Simone, I'm here to check on you. It's Jean." I can't begin to fathom why Jean Lafitte is outside my door. I never imagined he knew who I am or what my name is.

A few seconds pass, and I finally respond. "How can I help you?"

"Please, open the door," Lafitte purrs. "I just want to be of assistance to you, Simone."

The room stands still as I realize I have no choice.

Slowly, I open the door. I have to clench my fists to prevent myself from gasping. Despite all I have heard regarding Lafitte, I'm not prepared for having him in my presence. He is tall. I take one look at him and finally understand why he is so imposing. His hair is dark brown and brushes his shoulders, and his eyes are a piercing blue. Although he is no longer a young man, he still possesses the physique of a man who can handle the most physical of jobs. I hate to admit it, but I'm actually attracted to him. Quickly, I brush off my dress and look down the corridor.

"Please, come inside," I whisper. He smiles and brushes past me as he enters my room. *Now what?* I wonder. I have nothing to offer as far as food or drink are concerned.

I motion for him to sit on the only chair in the room. I definitely don't want him anywhere near my bedroom.

He sits in the chair and smiles up at me, as if he is trying to put me at ease. "How long have you been working here?" he asks. I take a deep breath and conclude that this is reality. I have to get it together.

"I have been at the hotel for a couple of years. It's good. I like it. I meet many different people." I become aware that I'm rambling. Lafitte nods as he soaks up each word that comes out of my mouth. We both go silent.

There is a shift in the room, and now Lafitte commands it. He stands up and walks over to me as he reaches for my hand. He is inches from my face, and we lock eyes. If the situation weren't so intense, it would seem as if it was part of a courtship.

"Simone, sit down for a moment. We need to talk."

At this point, I'm completely under his trance. I simply do as I'm told. I sit on the edge of my bed. (The place I don't want to be and where I feel the most vulnerable.) Lafitte crouches slowly in front of me, still holding my hand. "We have a slight situation. I feel I'm the only person who can tell you what I must tell you. We have both been betrayed by Thomas." I gulp and close my eyes as Lafitte continues.

"He has left you and stolen from me. After laying eyes on you, I cannot imagine how any man could think about leaving something as precious and lovely. His last words were that he would never be seen again. I tried, Simone. I called out to him, because, quite frankly, I knew he had a lot to lose. He said he had already met someone else, and my money was going to help ensure his future."

Suddenly, I feel short of breath. The room goes black, and I collapse to the floor and begin to shake. Tears sting my eyes, and I think I'm going to be sick.

"I'm so sorry. I wish I could say that none of this is true. Unfortunately, when I do find him, I will be forced to kill him. Thomas has been quite foolish." He reaches down to touch my chin, which is wet from tears. "I had to tell you."

Then Lafitte kisses the top of my head, stands up, and heads towards the door. I want him to leave. I want to be alone. I hear the door open. Thank God. Before the door closes, I hear the last words I will ever hear from Lafitte. "I'm sorry about the baby." The door closes.

It can't be. None of this can be happening. I have told no one about the baby. Thomas isn't really gone and never coming back.

I stay curled up in a fetal position for hours. My head pounds. The light of the new day is just beginning to peek inside my window. I stand up and notice that it is almost 6:00 a.m. My shift begins in an hour. Methodically, I fix my hair and change into my uniform.

I leave the security of my room and walk up the stairs. The winding staircase seems shorter this time, and the rooftop seems eerily quiet. Despite the breeze from the ocean, I can't hear a thing. I have always loved the waves and the calmness of the tides rolling in. I head toward the edge of the roof. It is a beautiful morning, and I walk until I no longer feel the roof's surface beneath my feet.

Jean Lafitte

The rain just won't stop. I probably should feel a slight pang of guilt about what I have just done, but I don't. None of this would be happening if people didn't double-cross me. After everything I have done for this crummy city and these worthless men! Thomas truly was like a son to me. I will not rest until I bring him absolute destruction. I would have thought that, after being by my side, he would have known not to pull something like this.

I finally see the lights ahead from the few remaining homes still operating in Campeche, my soon-to-be-extinct community. Oh, Campeche. It used to bring me warmth, but this place has turned into another Thomas, total betrayal. I'll get out of here, but on my terms.

Once I reach the steps of my beautiful red house, perhaps for the last time, I shake off my drenched coat. The water tumbles down my hat like a raging river. I don't enjoy feeling like a disheveled rat!

I don't bother with pleasantries. Obviously, time is not on my side. Between Thomas stealing all my hard work and an ungrateful city forcing me out, I have to think fast.

"Get me Evelyne, now!"

My favorite butler leaves on his mission without question. I guess I do play favorites. I have three servants whom I trust. Obviously, I can't trust my crew. I do my best, within reason, to shower these three with extra trappings that no one else would ever bestow upon them. After many years together, I believe there is a sense of loyalty, if not actual friendship.

I go straight into my parlor and throw everything off my desk. It's not like I'll need any of it now. As the papers, glasses, and lamps hit the wooden floor, I realize that this will soon be a distant memory. Once again, I will call somewhere else home.

"She's on her way," Caesar says. I look at him and nod. I have no time for small talk. My mind is racing, and I wonder what else

Evelyne might need. Ironically, she may be the most important person in my life. I have never traveled anywhere without her since the day I met her. She is an older lady who is directly related to Queen Marie Leveau herself. I wouldn't hire just anyone. Evelyne has always been instrumental in helping me with my most important decisions, whether involving finances, my health, or even love. Actually, she hasn't been quite as helpful in that last area. Some might question my belief in voodoo and black magic, but I would have to ask, "Are they Jean Lafitte?"

I will always remember the first time I stumbled upon the queen's doorstep. It was after a drunken night out, and I was with a group of questionable men. (After all, is there any group who is more fun?) They dared me to knock on her hidden door. No one dares Lafitte. After a few knocks, the door opened, and a stocky black woman with the most amazing headscarf stood on the other side.

"Can I help you?"

It was like love at first sight, if only she had been younger, slimmer, and more attractive. Still, our eyes met, and we clicked.

All I managed to say was, "I'm Jean Lafitte, and I want to use your services."

She gave me a once over before smiling broadly. "Well, why didn't you just say so?" Then I entered her mysterious home.

Over the years, I have used Queen Marie's help with numerous endeavors. The problem arose when I was being asked forcefully to leave South Louisiana and set up shop in Galveston. I don't know if it is just an issue with me, but I fear being alone. I proceeded to beg and even bribe Ms. Leveau, but she wasn't leaving her city. Finally, she came up with the idea of her older sister, Evelyne. Evelyne wasn't as charismatic as Marie, but she knew how to cast a spell. I was willing to give it a try, but I needed some reassurance first.

"Okay, Mr. Jean, what are you thinking?"

This could be a tough feat. After a few moments, I stirred up a desire within myself. I figured that should she be able to tell me what my newly thought-up desires were, she was the real deal. Evelyne closed her eyes for what seemed like an eternity before she tilted her head back to face the sky. She began to make a low-pitched humming noise, pressed her forefingers together, and then suddenly looked straight at me. "You are trying to steal some newer ships from Spain."

Enough said. I must admit I was entertaining the thought of obtaining a faster, sleeker ship. "When can you start?" I asked.

⁑ Fast Break

Ship channel, Modern Day,

It's been a long night, and I'm finally ready to dock. We are travel-ing through the Galveston Bay entrance and heading toward Eagle Point. I have been doing this same routine often enough that I know it like the back of my hand. Our ship's speed is now just ten knots, and she floats along easily. It is past midnight, and we pass only a few other vessels despite the heavy traffic that normally comes through on a daily basis. I make my way to the top, trying to get one quick look around before we end our journey. In the distance, I detect some lights. I get the feeling we aren't alone.

I'm winding down the exterior steps when someone from the crew begins cursing like a sailor (pardon the pun). "What is it?" I ask.

The heavyset man jabs a finger toward the looming lights. "Look at her! She's going way too fast!"

M L Rosynek

I spin around and notice that the once-far-away object is now rushing toward us. My feet seem glued to the deck as I watch the water splash violently. This is impossible. The night skies are clear. Suddenly, I hear voices from the engine room alerting us that water is beginning to flood important equipment. We all scramble as we prepare for more trouble. Then I hear something that causes me to freeze in my tracks. Besides the echoes of tornado-like winds circling us, I detect the distinct sounds of rickety wood. Instantly, our crew hits the deck, and the captain runs up from his cabin. He grabs his hat but loses his footing and slides over to the edge of the ship.

"Hurry, someone grab him!" I scream. Instinctively, we form a human chain and somehow manage to reach the shaken man's hand. "Hold on!"

I can't believe the shocking sight before me. The ship that was once so far away is coming straight for us. This can't be happening. However, not only is it happening, our situation seems dire. The oncoming object does not look like any modern-day vessel. It has huge sails and is made entirely of wood. If I didn't know any better, I could have sworn I just heard some creepy violin music and the sound of boards creaking while their crew walks around on the deck.

Our captain maneuvers himself to some dangling lights and flashes them toward the oncoming danger. It makes no difference now.

"Brace yourselves, men!" the captain yells. I grab the nearest pole and prepare for disaster. The other ship is going at least thirty knots and will impact us at any moment. It is true what is said about your life flashing before your eyes. Mine does.

I can tell by the sound of the waves crashing that the other ship is directly in front of us. It never even tried to change its course. Tip to tip, the two boats meet. Here we go.

Then, out of nowhere, the clinking of an old bell rings through the air, accompanied by the most bone-tingling noise I can imagine. Could it be? I identify the peculiar smell in the air as old, cheap rum, and then I hear laughter coming from the mayhem surrounding us. The chuckling feels as if the source is coming from deep inside a man's soul. A twisted man. The chuckling is motivated not by amusement but by sarcasm.

I have been too busy paying attention to the theatrics around us, and I fail to predict the increasing wind surges. It's too late. I fall flat on my back. I force myself into a sitting position and compel myself to take a deep breath. I look around and count heads, relieved to discover that everyone seems to be alive. Just one key element is missing from all this: the infamous ship that forced itself upon us. It appears to have literally passed right through us and disappeared!

Our captain rushes over, a worried look on his face. "I think we were just paid a visit by Jean Lafitte."

⁺⁺⁺ Alley-Oop

Arrival Day

Shea

Finally, summer has officially begun, and our week-long tournament will kick off our three months of freedom. I guess I must have dozed off somewhere on the interstate, because when I open my eyes, I see signs directing us into Galveston. I look around the car and notice that everyone else is still pretty much zoned out. Both my brothers are asleep, and Flynn, my best friend, is tapping his hands to the beat of his mysterious playlist. I overhear my brother, Matt, snoring in the backseat. He and I are only a year apart, which has made for some interesting moments. We have many of the same friends and have even overlapped some of the same girlfriends. I'm hopeful we will outgrow this particular stage, because it has made for some awkward dinner conversations. Currently, I have forbidden his latest crush to come over to our house.

I check my phone to see how many miles remain until we arrive at the hotel. According to Siri, we are only eleven minutes away. The itinerary is a bit more interesting for this particular trip. We are all booked at the Galvez. I hear it's pretty upscale, which I'm sure is code for "expensive." I search for the hotel on my phone. The pictures that pop up depict an historic-looking building complete with palm trees planted alongside a long circular drive. Evidently, it's one of the oldest hotels along the Gulf Coast. Personally, I'm just banking on it having free Wi-Fi and flat-screen TVs.

"Look. There it is. Cool," Andrew blurts. Andrew is my youngest brother and has boundless energy. I put my phone down long enough to notice a grand off-white building with a wrap-around terrace. The place does look pretty nice and, I enjoy a bit of luxury every once in a while. Actually, it's pretty fun to hang out with the team in a different environment. No matter how many hours spent sweating it out on a court, it's hard to understand the diverse backgrounds that all us come from. One guy had never even been to an Olive Garden before. He was so impressed that he begged our waitress for an extra pizza box to take home with him as a souvenir.

As we park the car, we tap into a renewed energy source and can't wait to hit the ground running. Unfortunately, this is one of the worst parts of a trip, because now the unloading begins. As I steer the luggage cart toward the awaiting doors, the only thought in my head is room service. The moment I hear the ocean, I begin to relax.

The closer I get to the hotel, the more I understand the magnitude of this place. I can only imagine what it must have been like during the last century. It must have been quite the experience staying in such a place. I can almost taste the salt in the air. It tastes good. I wonder which floor we will be staying on.

I glance behind me, checking out where everyone is, and something catches my eye on the roof. Several figurines are situated on top of the building. I can't make out what the statues are supposed to be, but they are impressive, and a bit intimidating. I have read about some of these buildings, and I assume their purpose was to help direct ships, back in the day. I remain transfixed on the roof for some reason, despite the sun attempting to burn my eyes. Just as I'm about to look away, I notice a young woman peeking out from behind one of the iron heads. Now, that is quite the dedicated worker. I'm not sure I would have the guts to climb all the way up there, Pledge in hand.

I watch the girl as she methodically wipes the cat-like creature's head. She's definitely into it. As I stare, I notice the girl is wearing a long dress. To each her own. Maybe she's supposed to be method acting some role for her job.

She notices me staring and stands up. I'm not sure if I should wave, smile, or just pretend I'm looking toward the beach. Before I can decide, she's gone.

"Shea, come on man!" Flynn shouts. I nod as if I'm agreeing, but I keep staring at the roof. I must be tired. I better remember to check my contacts, or my shot is going to be way off.

In the lobby, it becomes obvious that many famous people have stayed here. Up and down the hallway are photos of Frank Sinatra, Dean Martin, even FDR. I assume that, back in their day, they couldn't have imagined that this hotel would also be housing a bunch of basketball guys. I'm pretty certain that most of us know more about Steph Curry's latest three-point percentages than we do about history. I'll bet the old-timers didn't worry too much about their "handles."

I have my room key in hand. It says 501. Of course, we have to trek up five floors. The second floor would have been way too easy.

Matt, Andrew, and I hit the elevators and, as usual, argue over who has the honor of pushing the button. As the doors close, the last thing we hear is Flynn reminding us to meet up in thirty minutes for dinner.

The elevator is old fashioned and has wooden rails inside with an antique arrow showing which floor we are on. The arrow stops at "5," and the doors open slowly, revealing a hallway with a long oriental rug. Now the race is on for which one of us will get to the room first. After much wrestling around, we all wind up at room 500. "Next room," I say, as I point down the hallway. Matt is the first to arrive, and he has a rather confused look on his face.

"Where's the number? Is this it?"

I just shrug and swipe the room card. After the third time, I'm beginning to think maybe we do have the wrong room. Andrew is getting frustrated and manages to locate a maid at the far end of the corridor.

"Excuse me," Andrew says as he waves, trying to get her attention. "Can you tell us if we're at the right room?" The middle-aged lady leaves her cart and fumbles with her keys as she approaches.

"Thank you," I say. "Our card isn't working, and we aren't even sure this is the right room."

Without looking up, she assures us that we are, indeed, at the correct door. She swiftly swipes our card and, sure enough, the door opens.

"Sometimes this door can be tricky." She smiles. "Let me know if you need anything else." We thank her, and she is gone.

The room is really sweet, but for some weird reason, I feel a bit uneasy. I decide that the best way to shake it off is to check my Instagram. I pull out the Wi-Fi password. Nothing like a bit of modern technology to help erase this Old World feeling.

As Matt jumps into the shower and Andrew grabs the remote, I poke my head out the door to seek out the maid. I know she couldn't have gone too far. "I'll be right back. Don't lock me out, Andrew."

I don't see the maid, but I do hear some noises coming from the elevators. Maybe she's waiting over there. The noises grow louder the closer I get to the end of the hall, and I'm not sure what I'm hearing. It sounds like someone crying.

As I turn the corner, I see a young woman kneeling with her head in her hands. Great. I've never been good with girls and their tears. Somehow, I always manage to say the wrong things, but I can't just turn away. "Are you all right?" I whisper.

She seems to realize she is no longer alone, so she wipes her eyes before she slowly stands up. It's only then that I recall having seen her before. She's the young woman I spotted on the roof. Once again, I ask her if she's okay. She doesn't reply; just turns toward the elevator. I take it as my cue that she wants to be left alone. I doubt she wants a stranger interfering. This is awkward! I glance down at the carpet and then look up. I just need to make my way back to my room. Probably my best bet is to say a quick goodbye. Too late. She's gone. Again.

"Oh, come on!" Now I'm agitated. How on earth can I keep coming across this mystery woman?

I look in both directions, as if it will somehow explain what just happened. I feel a bit spooked, and sheer adrenaline takes over my body. I'm not standing here another second. I don't think I've ever run down a court so fast. The next thing I know, I'm banging on the door to our room. "Andrew! Open up!"

Andrew finally opens the door. "Bro, what's the deal? My gosh, you act like you've seen a ghost."

The last thing I want to do is answer Andrew's question. Pride and all. "Andrew, get ready. We're leaving for dinner and some amusement park in ten minutes." Andrew cocks his head to one side while looking at me for a few seconds too long. It's funny, but even little brother knows when to keep his mouth shut. This latest episode needs to be dropped now.

Our destination is called Pleasure Pier. It's much larger than I anticipated and is located on the seawall. It has too many little food joints and rides to count. I assumed the place was going to be similar to a traveling carnival, so I'm pleasantly surprised. I spot an upside-down roller coaster that suspends riders over the ocean and a swing ride that promises to elevate riders seventy feet into the air. Good times.

The first thing on everyone's mind is food. The choices are pretty obvious. It looks like it's going to be seafood, or maybe seafood. Something tells me I will soon be chowing down on some seafood. Our crew decides on Bubba Gump's, which happens to be advertising an all-you-can eat shrimp platter. They know us too well.

As we enter our chosen eatery, we strategically place ourselves directly under the giant screens, which are all airing the championship game. Luckily, the newfound ambience helps erase any recent memories of hocus pocus. I actually begin to relax and enjoy myself.

The time finally arrives when none of us can ingest one more shrimp. Next on the agenda is to get out of here and hit up as many rides as possible. As I grab my jacket, I can't help but notice a young boy staring at me. After a few moments, I glance over my shoulder, intending to give him a small shout-out. I blink a few times once I realize he isn't a child but a midget. I can't help but wonder why he's so fixated on our group. The young man appears to be in his early twenties and is decked out in full pirate regalia. He looks to be wearing a nametag indicating that he is an employee of Pleasure Pier. Instead of a heads-up wave, I flash him a peace sign as we leave the restaurant.

It's unusually cool for a May evening. I shouldn't be so surprised, because Texas weather is known to be unpredictable. As the old saying goes, if you don't like the temps, just wait fifteen minutes. The good news is that the night will be perfect for doing the rides. I've chosen to be the upstanding big brother and help chaperone Andrew and his friend, Dax. Dax is Flynn's little brother, but he isn't nearly as active as Andrew.

"Let's go for the log ride, Andrew," I say. Andrew and Dax explode into a full-out sprint, not letting up until they reach the end of the line. Never one to miss out on anything, Flynn decides to join us, and fifteen minutes later, we're sitting inside one of the wooden logs. The sky had grown darker, and the yelling surrounding us tells me this will be pretty cool. We are off and approaching our first descent.

Splash! Wouldn't you know it? I have managed to sit in the spot that splashes passengers the most, and I'm soaked! Flynn takes one look at me and bursts out laughing. I give a sarcastic response. I'm wringing out my clothes when I notice that the midget is sitting with us.

I'm trying to enjoy myself, but I'm a bit shocked to be sitting alongside this mysterious guy. What the heck? Flynn seems completely oblivious. His hands are raised high, and his lungs are working on overdrive. The swiftly moving logs reach the inevitable final drop, drenching all of us. I can barely feel my discomfort. I just want the ride to be finished. All in all, the event lasts maybe three minutes. We are channeled into the last chute as we prepare to set foot back on dry ground. I continue looking straight ahead, unsure if I should attempt to make small talk or not. It doesn't matter, because once Flynn notices our travel buddy, he begins the introductions. "Hey, didn't we see you at the restaurant? Dude, I love your outfit! Do you really work here?"

The diminutive pirate smiles slowly before answering. "I'm from Galveston. I couldn't help but notice you guys. I bet you're staying at the Galvez. Am I right?" He doesn't seem to be searching for an answer, and all his attention seems to be directed at Andrew. Andrew lets him know that his assumption is correct.

Our new tour guide exchanges some items with my little brother, and their talk soon turns to basketball. I can't seem to shake my uneasiness that our arrival to this island seems to be predestined. As I remain lost in my thoughts, the small employee, whose nametag says "Caesar," reaches into his brown waistcoat and pulls out several glossy brochures before shoving them into my little brother's hands. Andrew is excited to have more info regarding all the action promised in Galveston. Unlike the rest of my crew, my instincts keep nudging me to gather the troops and head back to the hotel. I manage to muster up the lame excuse of much-needed sleep for tomorrow's game, and the others take my cue. Before we leave, Caesar extends one last bit of hospitality, handing each of us a small bag of Pleasure Pier tokens.

"Thanks, man," I say.

A few hours after our experience at the Pier, I'm finally settled in my bed. I should feel really comfortable being surrounded by all the down pillows, but I'm not. What were the odds that a total stranger would become fascinated with us? While I would love to believe our chance meeting was nothing more than coincidence, I have my doubts. Oh well. I can't waste any more time on this matter. I'm tired, and I need to get some beauty sleep. No more thoughts of some strange underbelly world. I have some basketball to play. After all, hoops are a way of life.

‡ Block

Matt (*Morning One*) //

Unfortunately, I'm addicted to my phone, so much so that I admit to sleeping with my trusty device tucked under my pillow. This morning is no different. I'm still in a sleepy haze, but I'm already searching for my extra appendage. I roll onto my back and hold the phone mere inches from my face. I may be tired, but I can't help but notice the red bar is lit up. Ugh! I'm down to 2 percent. This is not good! I suppose that if there's a surefire way to get me out of bed in the morning, this is it.

Reluctantly, I get up and I search our room while trying not to wake my brothers. I would love a few extra minutes of peace and quiet.

I open suitcases and check tables that are littered with half-open Coke cans. Five minutes later, my patience has turned into sheer frustration. Where is that charger? The fact is, when you are one of three brothers, inevitably, there are fights. How can there not be? Don't get me wrong. We really do support one another, but no one can set me off like Shea or Andrew. If it isn't sports, it's girls or who got what for his birthday. We're all crazy competitive. Our phone chargers are sacred. I no longer care who I'm waking up or how loud I'm. In fact, I purposely become more obnoxious, tossing clothes onto the floor and slamming drawers as hard as I can, hoping at least one charger will magically appear.

"Seriously!" Shea shouts. "What the beep?"

"Where is my charger?" I snap. This situation is verging on full-out war.

"How would I know?" Shea asks.

I'm surprised it has taken Andrew this long to awaken from his slumber. He rolls onto his stomach while pulling the giant pillow over his head. He can be so dramatic. All it does is force me to grab the pillow and begin quizzing him about the possible whereabouts of the gadget in question.

I admit I'm singlehandedly starting our day on a truly low note, but I want my stuff. Shea stumbles out of bed and helps me look around the messy room. Deep down, even Shea understands that this lack of technology will affect him as well. We look in the bathroom, under the sofa pillows, behind the lamps, everywhere.

As we continue looking, someone knocks on our door. Shea and I break from our search, and I'm designated to see who wants our attention. I release a huge sigh after seeing a familiar face through the peephole. "It's Flynn," I say as I unlock the latch. Within seconds, Flynn stumbles into our little abode looking rather flustered.

"Dude, I woke up and couldn't find my phone. Of course, I blamed Dax, who denied everything. Whatever, but I decided to come down to your room just in case I left it with you last night, and look at what I found in front of your door."

Okay, I'll bite. I poke my head into the hallway, glancing down at the carpet. There they are, all in a neat little pile. Several phones tied up with even more phone chargers, displayed with a pretty little bow.

"Very funny! Who did this?" Part of me is relieved to have everything I need back in my hands, but the other part of me is beyond angry. Joke or no joke, this is pushing things too far. By this time, all four of us are wide awake, alert, and looking at each other with some hesitation. The look on their faces tells me no one knows how this happened.

I slowly shut our door and move toward the couch, feeling a bit nauseous. Breakfast isn't sounding as appealing as it did mere minutes ago. We all stare at each other. Silence.

"It's her. I know it is," Shea says. We don't answer him, just remain in our own thoughts. "We really need to find out more about that girl I saw. We need to know what her back story is."

Flynn jumps up nervously. "Shea, I don't care how hot you say she is, she's got some screws loose, as far as I'm concerned."

My new reality is becoming a bit surreal. Here the four of us are, discussing a bizarre event that just took place and not even questioning any of it. Shea looks a tad irritated. "She's a ghost. I don't think it has anything to do with her having a few wobbly screws."

Wouldn't you know it, there is more banging on the door. Flynn accurately predicts that the source of the noise will be Dax. "Come in," Flynn says. Dax darts inside and shoves his phone screen into Flynn's face. We all make a circle around the phone while Dax reads the message: "HELP ME."

Dax doesn't wait for any of us to offer explanations. "If this is some sort of joke, it's not funny!"

"Alrighty, then," Shea replies.

We agree a plan. Once again, the best strategy is always teamwork. Once we return from today's game, we'll take the hotel history tour. Information is knowledge, and knowledge is power. Anything we might learn about this mystery guest might help us explain some of the craziness we have just experienced.

As always, Andrew is the chosen wingman. He and Dax will beg our mothers persistently for tickets for the last time slot. I can't think of many people who want to put up with their nagging.

For the moment, I must try to focus on playing basketball. I have to block everything else from my mind. Instead of ghostly visions and bumps in the night, I must think about blocking shots and breaking ankles.

I get dressed and make sure I'm wearing all my good luck gear. I refuse to admit it, but I'm a bit superstitious. I always wear the same pair of underwear and socks and even shower in a certain order. I'm convinced that my ritual affects how I play. Maybe this is why I have resigned myself to believe that something unusual might be lurking on the fifth floor.

I take one last look into the bathroom mirror and then begin collecting my stuff. The first game of the day is against a team from West Texas. We should be able to beat them pretty handily. Good thing, because our next match might be tougher. I swing my backpack over my shoulder and head out the door.

The team is gathering downstairs in the lobby, and Shea and Andrew are already there. Once again, I'm running late. I press the "down" button in the elevator, and the light turns an amber shade. Luckily, the wait isn't long before the elevator doors open, revealing a twenty-something man who works for the hotel. We smile politely at each other, and he pushes a trolley into the elevator and then pushes the button for the lobby. It always seems awkward when enclosed with strangers inside these little boxes. Unlike what I normally do, I decide to make conversation. I'm not sure what comes over me, but the next thing I know I'm asking, "Have you ever experienced anything you can't explain since you started working here?" I keep my gaze on the floor numbers while awaiting an answer.

"Yes," the man replies a few seconds later. He gulps and looks at the ceiling. "Once, someone called the front desk, because their bathtub kept filling up on its own. Another time, someone called complaining that doors were slamming all night. It always seems to happen on the fifth floor, except for all the random toilet flushing in the lobby restroom."

I stand still, completely stunned. It looks like our hunches might be correct. I probably should have responded, because he becomes defensive. "I know what you're thinking. You think that I must be hallucinating or crazy. Never mind."

I can't just leave him hanging. "Is there a girl involved?"

The man reaches down for the wheels on the trolley. After readjusting a few things, he grabs the cart's shiny brass rails and pushes it out into the lobby. Before he disappears, he turns back to me. "You've seen her, haven't you?"

Shea *(Game One)*

Our first game is about to begin, and we're all getting loose on court one. Luckily for us, the gym is nice and new. The floors are shiny, which is good and bad. I can already guarantee that each one of us will be constantly wiping off the soles of our shoes as we play. The last thing I want is to provide additional entertainment for the people in the stands because I'm sliding around.

The game is well underway, and, as predicted, it has become nothing more than a glorified warm-up session. I glance around and notice that even the parents are more involved in their personal conversations than watching our shots.

Halftime comes and goes, and I find myself becoming a bit bored. I can't help but notice some of the spectators and players from various teams lingering around. The clock keeps ticking, and I force myself to remain focused. My mind inadvertently drifts off to tonight's ghost tour. Don't get me wrong, I enjoy a good fright and

even the occasional scream. However, tonight promises to be different. I'm hoping to uncover some answers. I may end up becoming a
true believer in all things unexplained.

"Shea!"

I twist around, throwing my arms up to my chest. Unfortunately,
my timing is way off, and the chest pass thrown at me heads out of
bounds. I'm grateful we're up by thirty. I begin to wonder if the ghosts
have followed me onto the court.

⁞ Press

Andrew (Night Two) ～～～～～～～～～～～～～～～～～～～～～～～

We finally return from the first day of play, and our plans for the night are looming closer. Forget today's game; it's ghost tour time. I just hope everyone appreciates all that I have to go through every day fulfilling their many demands. Of course, I locked the tickets. We all gather in front of an old picture waiting for our guide. I hope this is all going to be worth it.

The tour begins, but I'm already growing restless, bored even. Hanging at the back of the group, I decide to interject some of my own fun. As the procession heads down to the next hallway, led by some guy named Booker, I decide to work on some of my footwork and experiment with some backward shuffling. I take it one step further and imagine that I will be point guard to the oversized painting. I believe the guide said the wall hanging was someone named Bernardo. Let's see if Bernie can keep up with my moves. I pump my arms, so they're in sync with my feet and add a bit of side-to-side action.

I have always been taught to keep the mental game moving along with the physical. I decide to work on my focus skills and study the man in the painting while I keep moving. Bernardo has dark hair and a mustache. He reminds me of another dude I read about in history. All these people seem to wear frilly clothes with ruffles around their wrists. Personally, I wouldn't be caught dead in those threads. Bernardo's head is gigantic, which makes me think that King Lebron would look awesome hanging inside a large gold frame like this one. Soon, I'm thinking about my king wearing a Peter Pan collar with a glistening crown on his head. I feel like Mr. James would approve of his new image.

Eventually, even I'm finished with my experiment and decide to try locating my group. However, something catches my eye. It's Bernardo. I stand sideways, refusing to let some picture think it might be messing with me. Ever so slowly, I lean backwards, making sure not to look at him. Then, BAM! I jump up and face him. The serene stare I could have sworn he once displayed has been replaced with huge saucer-like eyes. Bernardo looks genuinely startled. I feel like I have him and begin waving my hands back and forth, preventing my worst enemy from throwing their pass inbounds. Here I am, jumping side to side, left to right. There's no denying it. It's plain as day that he is following my every move. Now it has become a full-blown game. I duck beneath him and notice his eyes searching for me. I jump out of view and see that he's looking in the direction he last saw me. Then it occurs to me that this game shouldn't be happening. How can it be occurring? Bernardo is an image on a canvas.

I must find the others. Sprinting down the hallway, I crash right into Matt. I can barely quit talking as I try to explain what just happened.

"Shh. . . . Not now, Andrew. You're being rude," Matt says. The only person who seems to realize something might be up is our tour guide.

Matt

I actually feel a bit sorry for the guide who has been assigned to take our crazy squad on this excursion. With our receipts in hand, we all make our way to the beginning of the hour-long ride, so to speak. It tips off in front of some old guy's selfie. The plaque on the bottom says, "Bernardo." Eventually, a chill-looking black guy walks up and announces that he is the chosen one for the evening. He introduces himself and says his name is Booker. He has the best looking flat-top and definitely hits the gym. He flashes a mega-watt smile and motions for us to follow him.

"We are gonna have a good time this next hour," he says with a grin. Booker is lit. "Since it's just us, let's have some quiet background music, just for mood." The next thing I know, I hear some classic B.B. King, courtesy of an iPhone. Booker teaches us the Cliff Notes version of Spain's arrival to the area and how Bernardo began this hotel. He gives us something else to chew on as he mentions that legend has it that Bernardo's eyes follow you, no matter where you're standing. This last fact causes all us to reach for our phones, hoping to take a quick snap. Who wouldn't want a pic for our latest posts?

The tour makes its way downstairs to the basement. We find ourselves standing in front of a "hall history." Everywhere I look I see photographs of eras gone by. Who knew Galveston was the site of the first Miss Universe pageant? That would have been a great way to meet girls! Although I must admit I'm not a fan of their swimsuit choices. The way people dressed back then would have been a challenge for me. I can't find a single pair of workout shorts in any of the pics. The women are even wearing long dresses on the beach. It all looks a bit too formal for my taste.

Eventually, Booker looks around, making sure he has everyone still with him. "Now, I'm certain you guys maybe don't understand, but back in the day, this was *the* spot. It had the sun, the sand, the partays!" Booker does a major dance move that would make Bruno Mars envious. "Just close your eyes," he continues. "There were the movie stars and presidents. It was wild, man." The soothing sounds of B.B. King are replaced by beats from Drake. I keep thinking that if some of my teachers would make their classes this interesting, I might actually study instead of using Google. I open my eyes and examine some of the things Booker just discussed.

"What about the ghosts and stuff?" Andrew asks.

Booker gives him a sly smile and walks over to him. "Hey little man. You curious about all that?" He tousles Andrew's hair as Andrew nods. Secretly, I'm curious too. "All right then," Booker says. "You know, yeah, people say they've seen and heard some stuff." I try playing it cool, but some of this talk is freaking me out. I don't even want to go to the bathroom alone anymore.

"What about you, Booker?" Andrew asks.

Booker shrugs. "I don't know. Hey, we have one more hallway."

The next hall is filled with even more photographs, mostly of old gangsters. Wouldn't you know it, Booker has the soundtrack from *The Godfather,* and now it's drowning out our small talk. After a few more minutes, he shows us to the back patio. *The Godfather* beats segue into heavy bass from *Jaws.* (I'm sensing that our tour guide's sense of humor is a bit twisted.) I decide to hang back a bit and keep reading about these infamous mobsters. I overhear someone from the team quizzing Booker about a basketball tattoo they spot underneath his pant leg. Evidently, the ink says, "Ball is life." I could have told them that!

I laugh to myself when I stumble across an old sketch of a pirate surrounded by a pack of large black hounds. If only Andrew had noticed the image.

I'm about to go outside when one black-and-white image causes me to stop. It depicts a group of men standing around a giant Christmas tree. They are holding drinks, and there is a piano in a corner. I assume carols were being played, and it was a fun time. A small notation on the bottom corner states that the year is 1900. What catches my eye is not the scene itself but the participants. The young man smiling front and center is none other than Booker. How is that possible? The photograph is supposedly from over one hundred years ago!

I try frantically to scoot by everyone, hoping to get Shea's attention. "Shea!" I hop a few inches off the floor, motioning for him to rejoin me. Any other time, I doubt my brother would have been so accommodating. However, considering recent events, Shea walks toward me. Instead of trying to describe what I have just seen, I merely point to the picture in question. Then we both turn and head outside. Booker is holding the door for us, and he gives us a wink.

Shea

Matt and I are out on the back terrace and have joined all the others. After some quick small talk, we agree to meet up at the pool. Being typical guys, we tease each other about who gets first dibs on any cute girls who might happen to be there. Naturally, there is some light-hearted digs aimed at anyone who missed an open layup before we all leave for our rooms. In the meantime, Matt and I make sure Flynn witnessed what we both did. Needless to say, Flynn is speechless. There's a first time for everything.

"Listen," I say, "I really think if we're going to sort out what's been happening, we have to go directly to the source—Booker—and ask him, what the . . .."

If all the latest info wasn't enough, Matt goes into detail with Flynn regarding Andrew's one-on-one session with Bernardo. I decide to point out the obvious and remind them that Booker even winked at us. Let's face it; Booker is in on the joke. Flynn heaves a huge sigh, and I expect both of them to balk at my proposal. Instead, I'm shocked when Matt says, "Let's go."

The grand Galvez is set up in such a way that, despite our being under eighteen, we can still grab a small round table near the main bar area. The venue seems to encourage guests to slide up a chair and join in the fun. The dark mahogany bar situated in the center appears to be the same bar from the historical photos. Not much has changed. As we sit there, I imagine Frank Sinatra seated nearby wearing his impressive sports jacket surrounded by his posse. Sinatra had his team, just like we have ours.

The three of us are sitting together, but no one speaks speak. Our questions don't make any sense, but none of us can deny what we have seen. Another ten minutes go by, and I'm about to give up, but then I spot Booker coming out of the kitchen. He's carrying a little notepad, and he comes over to greet us. "I'm gonna pretend you're all of age," Booker says, laughing. "What can I get ya?" The three of us face our eager waiter while holding our gazes a bit longer than we should have.

"Answers," I respond.

Maybe we were expecting some type of denial from Booker or, at the very least, a confused look. But when it comes to Booker, he doesn't beat around the bush. He looks around as if he's wondering who might overhear our conversation. Slowly, he shifts his weight back and forth while adjusting his tie. Booker must have felt the urgency in our voices, because he forges straight ahead. "It's the picture. I saw the look in your eyes." We all stare at him before he blurts, "I've aged well, huh?" He bends down and adds, "It's the Botox."

Okay. Now my head hurts. How can any of this be happening? Surely, there is some mistake. Maybe the plaque is a misprint. Matt plays with his phone before sitting on his hands. I can tell he's growing increasingly nervous. Flynn's eyes are dilated to the size of a deer facing oncoming headlights. (I happen to know what that looks like, being from the Texas Hill Country.)

"Move over there," Booker instructs as he points to a secluded table. We decide it's simpler to just do what he says. As we make our way over to the new spot, it seems odd that none of us is afraid. I'm experiencing many emotions right now, but fear is not one of them. Still, as much as I have enjoyed meeting our new "old" friend, I recognize he is from another dimension. We watch as Booker closes all his tabs and removes his perfectly starched vest before hanging it on a hook behind the bar. He checks his phone and then slides a chair over to join us. My stomach is in turmoil. I keep wishing I hadn't wolfed down three spicy burritos on the way back from the gym.

Once seated, Booker asks, "Who's first?" So many questions are spinning through my mind. Who exactly is the hot little drama queen who keeps showing up at the most inopportune times? Also, what about that Caesar guy from the Pier?

Before I know it, Matt asks, "That picture was you, only it's not possible." Booker spins his chair around and throws his legs over the sides. Nothing seems to fluster this guy. At this rate, we could go on and on and play all sorts of mind games with one another. It all sounds so irrational, but somehow, we all know that the weirdness going on is true.

"Booker, man, just be straight with us," I say. "We aren't out to get anyone in trouble or start any kind of drama."

I don't know if it's my heartfelt plea or my direct eye contact, which is now bordering on stalker status. Maybe he just feels sorry for me, but he decides to spill. Booker's playfulness transforms into a much more serious tone. He places his almost-empty bottle of water on the table in front of him. "Well, I guess you could say I have lived a full life. I have definitely lived through some serious trends. I quit celebrating my birthday sometime last century. I started losing track of how old I really am." He laughs to himself. We just keep sitting there. I dare not interrupt him for fear that he will stop speaking.

"But how? I mean, are you, you know, like, a ghost?" Flynn asks. If Booker is a ghost, I think I might understand all this a bit more. He must be like the mysterious babe who isn't quite present.

I straighten up quickly and snap my fingers as if my team just won 2K. "You're like the girl!"

As my crew nods enthusiastically, Booker brings us all back down to earth. "What? Wait, no, man. Simone?" He breaks out laughing and looks down at the water bottle. "She's dead. Like, for real, that girl is dead. You know what I'm saying? She could be the lead actress in Ghost Hunters or something." At this point, our bubbles are burst, and we're entirely confused. As Booker regains his composure, I become annoyed. He must sense my displeasure, because he says, "Man, come on. Don't be like that. I want to show this clan something." He gets up and motions for us to follow him into the lobby. Sensing our uncertainty, Booker tilts his head back. "I ain't kidding, you wanna know or not?" We all follow him.

Ever so quietly, walking in single file, we exit the world of cocktails and enter the storied world of history. First up is Bernardo. I'm a bit taken aback when I notice Booker going into the lobby restroom instead of staying put in front of the Spaniard. Did our tour guide drink one too many? Somehow, our group manages to squeeze into the well-maintained bathroom, and Booker reaches behind us, securing the lock. I suppose this means business. Without offering any explanations, Booker enters one of the two stalls and swings the hinged door open with his foot, keeping it wide open with his free hand. While I'd love to inform him that this is an activity meant to be done in private, I get the feeling that our being here has nothing to do with bodily functions. I feel one of my eyebrows rise, and Booker takes the bait. "These toilets are much more than what you think. They might as well be American Airlines. The rumors of excess flushing hold more weight than you understand. This is essentially how I got here."

I knew there was much more to the flushing noises than anyone was letting on. No one needs to use the bathroom that much. Maybe it's just that all us are guys, but I did notice a bit more action in a public restroom than usual, especially in a nice hotel. Is it really too much to ask that some of these people could just head up to their rooms to do their business?

As I try wrapping my head around this absurd situation, Booker attempts to clarify it. "You asked me if I was a ghost. Heck no! I chose to come here, and I choose to stay. The bottom line is that some of us in this city are not exactly new to the area, understand? It's just that once we crossed over, so to speak, we stay the same. Well, we stay with the styles, though, man." He laughs. "It's a portal, guys. I wanted out. I escaped that night. You know, from him, Jean Lafitte, and I'm not the only one. There are others."

Andrew freezes. "It's like that Narnia movie, but without the lion. Who else?"

Booker's face transitions into a wide smile, and he reaches over for Andrew. For the first time, I notice a tiny tattoo on the inside of his wrist. I squint to make out the markings. Instead of the usual artwork, the tattoo seems otherworldly.

"What's that?" I ask. Booker releases Andrew's hands while simultaneously turning his own wrists over. "Property. I was his property. He liked to place his initials on us, like we were his pets, only he liked his pets more." Despite how illogical all this sounds, it is beginning to make some sense. Booker escaped one night long ago and came over to a new side, a fresh start. Unlike the girl, he isn't a ghost. I just have to clarify a few things.

"Are you implying that this so-called portal happens to be a toilet? If that's the case, why does it only work sometimes? And where is the other side of this puzzle?"

At this point, Booker seems to be in a daze. I get the feeling our discussion of past events might be bringing up some inner sorrow and pain. Why us? I can't help but wonder. Why, after all these years, is our little group the catalyst for resurrecting history? Sure, some of this is exciting, but it must be a painful recollection for those who lived it. Unfortunately, I get the impression that to advance to the next chapter, a dark chapter must be sufficiently closed once and for all.

Matt

I will never look at a toilet the same way again. I can even go one step further and add that I don't think I will be able to watch a bathroom cleaner commercial without having some serious trepidation. While hordes of unsuspecting hotel guests are making random visits to the bathroom and downing drinks at the pool, they have no idea there is a slight chance they might be sucked back and forth between the present day and the past. Did I mention that the past includes a murderous pirate? I mean, really, who knew?

"First of all, why some bathroom fixture? I mean, that's gross and disgusting, you know?" I ask our old friend. Booker explains that the portal wasn't always a toilet. It has changed over the years. Evidently, it is the vicinity that matters. Booker takes it many steps further and reminds us about the extent of Jean Lafitte's fascination with magic and voodoo.

"Evelyne, that was her name, and she was by far the most important person in that man's life. I'll tell ya, at first, even I was skeptical, but I began seeing things with my own eyes. She did some crazy spell and, *poof*, the stuff really happened. She created the portal that night. She may have been on Lafitte's payroll and given him bank by using her gifts, but she wasn't gonna leave us all stranded there."

Man, I wish I could have been a fly on the wall that evening. Booker describes the frightened crew sprinting toward the water's edge hoping to jump onto any available ship. We are all engrossed by the details of cover-up and survival. As the tale grows more sordid, the truth is slowly exposed regarding the lingering hotel chambermaid and her never-ending evening strolls.

Booker chuckles. "You must have seen Simone. She probably finds you guys kind of cute. She's a flirt." I'm just linking the name to the image of the floating wannabe *Sports Illustrated* model when Booker explains that they are one and the same. "Simone was, or is, I don't know, a beautiful young woman. She can be a pest at times. All her pacing around. Girl definitely has her moods. At the hotel, we've just learned to put up with her. One time she was so angry with me that she took it out on all our lady guests. She's a jealous one, that girl. Maybe it's her Latin genes."

"Can you explain a little more about what happened to Simone?" Flynn asks.

"Oh, sorry," Booker says, seeing our confused looks. "Simone lived back in the day when this hotel was built. I'm talking back in the heyday of Lafitte and the pirates. Didn't you study all this in school? Galveston was once a huge hub for pirates. Unfortunately for Simone, she fell madly in love with a young privateer. He was Lafitte's right-hand man, but things didn't work out the way she was hoping. The legend goes that Simone had just found out she was with child. Her baby's daddy was a young pirate named Thomas. He was from here and had gotten himself hooked up with Jeal. Sorry, we call Lafitte "Jeal." Look at it as the man's rap name. I coined it over the last decade or so. Anyways, Thomas loved her; there's no doubt about it, but he also loved money. Lafitte loved money. Thomas decided to do his own bit of double-crossing the last night they were all here on the island. Plain and simple, Simone was collateral damage."

"What happened? What happened to Simone?" Flynn asks. Suddenly, this story is becoming the most amazing campfire tale we have ever heard. Flynn and I are in a trance.

"You have to understand," Booker continues, "back in the day, Jean Lafitte was like a glorified rock star. Sure, he was technically a crook, but the people loved him. What wasn't to love? He was crazy handsome and basically gave away all these amazing stolen goods to people who never would have been able to afford them otherwise. Even the American government needed his help, what with all his ships and money. The problem is, when things are that good, inevitably, they're going to go bad."

"What about Simone?" I ask.

Booker realizes he's been sidetracked. "Simone was Thomas's fiancé and the daughter of your favorite piece of artwork, Bernardo." He points to the infamous painting of the man himself. "It was like the perfect storm, if you will. That evening, Lafitte had to leave Galveston. Heck, he was literally being thrown out. Then he discovered that Thomas, who was like a son to him, was taking off with all the loot. Lafitte was always going after the Spanish; Bernardo was Spanish." Booker stops and shakes his head. "Those two supposedly hated each other. I guess, looking back, it was a bit of a revenge thing. Lafitte had to have the last word."

"What did he do?" Flynn and I ask in unison.

"No one will ever know for sure, but at some point, he ended up here at the Galvez knocking on Simone's door. Once the doomed girl answered, Lafitte told her that the love of her life had left for good. I imagine she felt like she couldn't go on."

Everyone ceases talking, and I feel a pain in my stomach. If that really was Simone that I saw, imagine the never-ending sorrow. Wow.

Booker attempts to infuse our tense situation with some much-needed comic relief. "She can be a real pain in the . . . you know what I mean. Drama! But we really do love her. She has become the unspoken ambassador of our home here. Truthfully, most of us hope she will find her inner peace and be able to move on someday, ya know?"

Gosh. She's still pretty hot. At least the girl floating around is hot. Games aside, I understand what Booker is saying. It would be awesome if there was a chance for Simone to reconnect with that Thomas guy. My thoughts trail off.

Flynn shakes me out of it when he asks, "What's Bernie's deal?"

Booker stands up and straightens the creases that have formed in front of his pockets. "Bernardo is still here. Maybe he just doesn't want to leave his daughter behind. He's a joker." I sense our conversation is drawing to a close. "You know, you should go out back and visit Simone's shrine. Maybe she'll try talking to you."

With that, Booker leaves the room.

⁝ Rebound

Shea *(Middle of the Night)*

I have been tossing and turning all night. As much as I want to get some sleep, I can't stop thinking about the conversation that Flynn and I had with Booker. It would be impossible to comprehend if not for our sightings of Simone. I force my eyes shut, hoping my body will go totally Zen, to no avail. The sounds of Matt and Andrew snoring forestall my attempts at sleep. Just then, I remember the adjoining door between my room and Flynn's. Maybe I'm not the only person who is unable to rest.

Ever so slightly, I crack open the door a few inches and poke my head through. Wouldn't you know it, Flynn sits upright, as if he's been anticipating my entrance. He gets out of bed and gestures toward the hall. I should have known Flynn was going to be prepared for something different this evening, because he whips out his KD glasses and is wearing his UIL championship shirt. Flynn is dressed for a workout. "Let's do some exploring," he says with a grin. Somehow, I knew he was going to say that.

I remember to grab a key card before we sneak out. We're definitely living dangerously. Forget Simone and Bernardo. If my mom discovers me missing, we'll be in for it. Luckily, her room is situated directly across the hall.

Flynn bypasses the elevators and heads straight for the stairs, and we descend toward the lobby. "Where are we headed, exactly?" I ask. I take one look at my friend and recognize that he's as pumped as ever. I just hope he can muster up some of this energy during the tournament.

"The shrine. Let's find it," he replies. I was afraid he'd say that. Part of me was hoping to remain inside the safe confines of my room. I find myself constantly checking behind me, as if I'm expecting someone to approach me at 2:30 a.m.

We do our best to remain silent as Flynn grasps the door, which opens to the long, winding pathways that lead guests out to the beach. The only sounds I hear are distant waves and some trees that make snapping noises, as if on cue. I'm fairly certain this place is rather serene during daylight hours, but at this hour, it's a bit unnerving.

"Now where?" I ask. We stop and look up at the looming roof of our hotel. "I hate to be macabre, but wasn't she walking toward the water? I'm thinking that end." I point in the most likely direction.

We creep through the bushes and manicured landscaping. I doubt management was planning on any of their guests needing to go off the beaten path like we are. As soon as we're within earshot, I notice the corner of a flimsy metal fence. The contrast between the grandiose building and the hidden wire fence is a bit jarring. Flynn and I have arrived at the back of the building. It is apparent that not many others have made their way to where we are standing.

"Is this the spot where she fell that night?" Flynn asks. We take a closer look inside the enclosed area and see some dried-up flowers scattered around the grass. I think we have our answer. We remain still while taking it all in.

I never knew Simone, but she evokes some type of emotion inside me. I can't wrap my head around why she would want to stay grounded to a place that has caused her so much pain. I would think that by now she has heard that Thomas really did love her. I'm replaying the words out of Thomas's mouth, detailing all the tragic events that occurred that infamous evening. It must have been overwhelming, especially because Simone opted to end her life. I'm feeling that Flynn is absorbed in similar thoughts, and we both walk over to the other side. Neither of us dares say a word, and it feels like we're invading someone's innermost sanctum. A few more seconds pass before the heaviness of the moment gives way to the distinct sounds of a foot stepping on dry leaves.

"What was that?" Flynn whispers. We hear the sound again. We are definitely not hearing things. Something is causing the bushes to act like they are possessed. "I swear, Shea, if that chick comes anywhere near me, I'm screaming for dear life! I don't care how good she looks. I like my women alive!"

The subtle sounds grow louder. This is not funny. I feel a chill. I can't determine if the drop in temperature is due to an unexpected burst of wind or the lack of blood going to my extremities. The next few words out of my mouth might be expletives. Neither of us moves a muscle as we stare at the shrubbery in question. Then the bush screams at us as it is seemingly parted down the center. "Ahhhhhh!" My pent-up emotions morph from sheer terror to absolute irritation. It's Andrew and Dax!

Andrew runs full speed straight toward us and leaps onto me. We fall hard to the ground. Flynn finds it in him to muster up a good laugh and then joins in on the wrestling match. I, on the other hand, am not happy. "Andrew, what are you doing here? How did you even know where we were?"

Andrew stops long enough to sit up. "Because we've been spying on you. Seriously, Dax and I don't even get to play in this tournament. We need something to do." My instant reaction is to give him the evil eye, but he has a point.

"Well, let's all get back inside."

Luckily, our room key works right away. Andrew cozies up by my side. "Shea, please don't be mad," she says shyly. "We want to help. Besides, we found something that you might want to see."

I'm trying to be understanding, but I don't really want my little brother joining me on my latest expedition. The four of us are climbing the exterior stairs when Andrew interrupts us again. "We saw a picture of the real Simone. She looks just like the girl you saw in the hall."

We all slip back to the safety of our respective beds. If anyone would have told me a couple of days ago that I would be encountering the supernatural or having conversations with centuries-old people, I would have called them certifiable. I almost forget the real reason we're in Galveston, to play some basketball. I must get to sleep! I can only operate on nerves and frappuccinos for so long. It isn't exactly the healthiest of combinations.

As I tuck myself back into bed, I try to shut out all recent distractions. My eyes get heavy, and my breathing becomes deeper.

I must have fallen asleep, because I'm jolted upright with the clock now displaying 3:30. The red digital numbers keep flashing and are causing a hint of light inside the room. I sense I'm not alone. Inching toward the headboard, I never release the security of my comforter. I'm petrified to look at what might be staring back at me from the other end of my bed. I decide to suck it up and take a quick glance. Sitting at the end of my covers is none other than the star of our show, Simone.

I know I should be scared, but once again, I'm not. We stare at one another for almost a minute before I feel the need to engage in some actual communication. I notice that her long hair is pulled over one of her shoulders, and she has the semblance of a smile on her face. I guess this is a good thing when dealing with someone who is not alive. I'd like to think our interaction will be positive. She appears somewhat bashful, nervous even. I can barely manage any words but decide to try reassuring her that she has nothing to fear. "Simone."

The semi-seated mirage elevates several feet into the air. I remind myself that it is highly doubtful that this girl will behave in the same manner as the girls I know from school. Whatever I do, I don't want to scare her off. I reach behind me and tap on the wall a few times, hoping to get Flynn's attention. Seriously, how many occasions does one have to converse with a ghost?

Luckily, Flynn takes the bait and barges into my darkened room. He appears jittery, and his shirt is on backwards. It appears that he may have gotten more sleep than me. Before I can get the words out of my mouth, Flynn recognizes my new roommate. He keeps shifting his eyes back and forth between me and the "hot girl." Simone's white dress is a bit transparent, but not in an erotic way. A subtle scent of magnolias permeates the room. Obviously, she isn't exactly a great romantic prospect for me or Flynn. Still, I feel an obligation to try and help her.

"She acts a bit obsessed with you." Flynn is many wonderful things but politically correct is not one of them. I have a gut feeling that Flynn could have said many things not to upset her. These words weren't the ones.

Simone glides a few inches above the floor and begins to circle me. If I had any doubt about whether she was an apparition, I don't anymore. Her semi-mortal figure morphs into a leaner, slinkier serpent shape, complete with her flowing hair. She encompasses me like a constrictor would do to its prey. The big difference is that this isn't an episode of *River Monsters*.

I'm frozen in fear. Flynn reaches out to me, but his hands go right through her. I seem to be stuck inside her crazy ghostly grip. She slithers faster and faster. I have to figure something out, and now!

"Simone, I have a girlfriend!" The statement is false, but it puts all the current motions on permanent pause.

Matt and Andrew finally take notice and sit up, rubbing their eyes as Simone's snake-like outline gradually returns to her original feminine form, but the once-innocent look that was on her face has all but disappeared. She floats backwards and glances out the window. Before we understand what's happening, the electricity in the room goes off, and we're enveloped by darkness. I search for my phone, hoping the light will give us some pause, when suddenly we're blinded by the reddest sparks any of us have ever seen. It really is a shame that the red lights happen to be Simone's eyes. The intensity of her stare causes a slight burn on my face.

"What's wrong with her? Stalker!" Andrew shouts.

Poof! The numbers on the digital clock begin flashing again, and the TV turns on. Simone is gone.

At this point, I'm so done, I can't take any more. "We'll reconvene in the AM," I say. With that, the four of us go straight to sleep.

⁑ Man to Man

Andrew *(Morning Two)*

What a night! I take an early morning stroll on the beach to snap myself out of my current funk. The truth is, I'm restless. My gut tells me not to venture out alone, but my legs continue walking. It is early and still dark. The only real light I have to work with is coming from the Tiki torches located sporadically along the shoreline. Despite it being such a busy week on the island, the stillness around me is disturbing. I forge ahead and don't stop until I reach an enclave of trees. Do I go ahead and walk down the tiny path, which offers no immediate hope for some daylight, or do I stay relatively safe and predictable? This is a no-brainer. Dark path it is. I might as well go for it.

As I continue my informal hike, I grasp the glossy pamphlets Caesar gave me the other night. I pull one out, hoping it will keep me company on my journey. No sense in being lonely.

The bold red lettering on top describes an evening pirate trip that can be had for just $50 per person. Of course, a feast fit for a true adventurer will cost an additional sum. As I read the details, I can't help but recognize that the sketch on the front of the pamphlet is of the same drawing that is prominently displayed along the hall of history back at the hotel. The man in question is sporting a three-day-old beard and is accompanied by a pack of black dogs. One of the man's perfectly arched brows is raised a bit higher than the other, and his hands hold the lead canine's leash. I stare even harder and find myself feeling sorry for the poor beast, because his neck seems to be bulging from beneath the leather confines of his leash. Geez, you'd think the illustrators could have eased up a bit on their drawings. I almost get the feeling that I'm somehow connecting to the animal and find myself scratching around on the artwork. I have no idea what possesses me to do this, because it's just a picture, after all. Still, his eyes look so sad.

After a few more seconds, something peculiar happens. The dog's eyes blink. I respond in kind. The dog's eyes blink again. I find myself looking around, wondering what I'm seeing. Then, as if mere eye contact isn't enough, the dog's mouth opens slightly, and I'm almost certain I hear a low-grade growl. That's it! Instinctively, I drop my reading material and jump backwards.

Big mistake! The formerly sweet-looking pets methodically poke their huge, furry paws out of their 2D world, one at a time. First, I see a bunch of fur pushing through the glossy paper, followed by a toenail. Yes, it is most certainly a black dog paw working its magic into my 3D existence. I have definitely seen enough. I'm out of here!

How is it possible that I can go to bed one night dreaming of Steph Curry's latest half- court shot, only to wind up the next day running for my life? Don't get me wrong; I've watched enough scary movies on Netflix to have felt a true scare or two, but nothing compares to what I'm experiencing. My feet are going so fast that I don't even know why I haven't passed out yet. I choose not to look back for fear that I might see what's chasing me. The last time I checked, I saw many dogs with no evidence of any obedience school training. I'm not sure if they are Labs or wolves, but I'm certain their heavy breathing is getting much closer. I could have sworn I just felt some disgusting drool hit my calf.

Unfortunately for me, one of the pesky critters is a bit faster than the rest of the pack. Like any seasoned athlete, now is the moment I must implement my six years of training. Who does he think he is? I dart back and forth along the beach, imagining that I'm running lines. Instead of running toward a goal, I head toward the water. I'm getting closer to the shoreline, but then I decide to deke out the dog, demonstrating my full-court press.

I turn and face my opponent. I may not be holding a ball, but I can still distract the thing with some great ball-handling skills. It seems to be working, because I hear the dog pant even louder. I crouch and have him eye to beady eye. "You want some of this? Let's go!"

My court moves go on for a little longer before the animal finally hits the sand hard. He pulls himself up just in time for my final amazing move. Instead of shuffling from side to side, I plow straight ahead. I have done this trick many times before. The goal here is that when I come to a sudden stop, the opponent does not. True to form, it works. The dog goes down one last time and doesn't get back up. "Crossed up!"

I hear a slight whimper coming from the broken animal and feel a twinge of guilt. After all, a dog is supposed to be man's best friend. No longer able to hear or see the rest of the pack, I stand over my locked-up adversary. As I look down at him, his black eyes soften, and he rolls over onto his back, displaying his stomach to me. Am I supposed to rub his belly, like a real pet?

Wait a minute. I refuse to be deceived by magic or trickery. I keep expecting something ominous to appear. I turn around, searching for any sign of impending danger. Nothing. Then I make the mistake of looking down at my feet and see the dog looking up at me with all four legs extended in the air. All I can think about is how scared the poor little guy is feeling. (Maybe "little" isn't the most accurate description.) I bend over and rub his belly, and the dog licks my hand.

"Come on. Let's get out of here." The animal rolls over and jumps up. The two of us walk back to the hotel as if we're old friends. "You really do need to work on your moves. Conditioning will help. You have the attitude though. That's a good thing, Russell. From now on, you're the resident Russell Westbrook of the team." Russell's tail waves high in the air as he happily follows me back. I guess you really never know when you'll find your new best friend.

The two of us continue walking until we see lights flickering around the pool. It dawns on me that I have not really thought out my Plan B, so to speak. I have no idea how I'm going to get this dog upstairs into our room. It may only be 7:00 a.m., but several people are already scurrying around the pool, hoping to secure their favorite lounge chairs for the day. I wonder if I'm being too obvious. No worries. I take refuge behind a potted plant. I've concluded that Russell really is filled with some magic dust, because he waits by my side without making a sound.

"Andrew, are you bored, man?" It's Flynn. He sure is a sight for sore eyes. His upbeat attitude quickly evaporates when he sees who I'm with. "Are you serious? Is that one of those ghost dogs?"

I would hate to think that I have just gone through what I have just gone through, only to fall short of my ultimate goal. I explain everything to him in record time while still escaping everyone else's prying eyes. Flynn reminds me that my biggest battle will come when I pack Russell up for the inevitable car ride home. *First things first,* I think. We scoot up the stairwell unnoticed as Russell gives me a wet sloppy kiss. Loyalty.

⁝ Backdoor

Daniel (Game 1)

Luckily, I have a small break between games. This will enable me to go scout out a few out-of-town teams that I've been hearing about. Evidently, there's some group from the Hill Country that are said to hold their own. My inside man, Booker, texted me about them. I find a spot in the stands and take some mental notes regarding a few of their plays. They seem to work together as a team. I'm stoked. Competition is a good thing. If we end up playing them, it should be a good game.

The game goes back and forth for a few runs, but then their team pulls out to a comfortable lead. It's time to gather my stuff and head back to my own court. I shove everything inside my backpack, reach down for my water bottle, and throw my jacket over my back. As I stand up and begin to walk down the sidelines, I notice one of their guys pull up and stare at me. Does he know something that I don't?

Shea (Night Three)

Today's game went pretty much as expected. It was a fairly easy win, but I'm sure the successive rounds won't be such a cakewalk. We rid ourselves of a day's worth of sweat and then head downstairs for an impromptu meeting with Booker. It's becoming apparent that not only is the local time traveler an ardent hoops fan, he is also fairly friendly with some of the local talent. Note to self: despite his fondness for us, I'm not sure where his tournament loyalties lie.

This particular get-together takes place on the sand right outside of the hotel's walkway. As I kick off my shoes, I notice the distinct smell of chocolate in the air. Thank heavens for hotels and their love of s'mores. The good news is that it appears that none of us will have to venture too far to score some serious carbohydrate loading. After all, the muscles hurt!

Booker is the last one to secure himself a spot in the sand, and he doesn't bother with a beach towel. "My man, Daniel, watched you losers play today. Believe it or not, he was impressed." He grins.

"He better be," I respond. Just as I'm easing into a jovial mood, the atmosphere shifts when Booker describes the rest of his conversation with the local standout.

"He had a strange dream, or should I say a nightmare." Booker goes on to describe a vision that Daniel had of Simone screaming as she was left to levitate indefinitely, because her final steps the last evening never ended. The image leaves me spooked. I can only imagine what it must have been like seeing that all night long. If I didn't know any better, I'd be inclined to believe the girl needs some serious closure.

Andrew

Wow! All the while, I thought an episode of *Gravity Falls* was strange. The stories I'm hearing blow all those out of the water. I understand I may be the youngest person here, but I'm overcome with an idea that might help bring this crazy rap song to its last beat. Sometimes, I feel that people don't give me enough credit, except for on the boards. Believe it or not, I understand what all this is about, at least as much as they do. I feel as if we can truly help this girl. I still don't understand why I'm continually forced to explain myself. "We can at least try reuniting Thomas with Simone," I say. The entire crew looks at me as I wait for one of them to tell me, yet again, what a stupid idea I had. What is it with these guys sometimes? After a brief silence, I'm stunned by the reply.

"Actually, Andrew might be onto something," Flynn says. "Everyone deserves their 'happily ever after.'"

Booker contemplates this idea as he slips off his shoes and tucks his feet beneath him. Flynn stands up and pats Booker on his back. "Well, what do you think?"

Booker remains silent as he rubs the distinctive ink on his wrist. Never one to remain on one sinister topic for too long, he shifts the focus back to the original question. After what seems like an eternity, he mumbles, "I like it. Let's do it." We respond with a deep, collective sigh as we begin preparing for our biggest splash yet. Let's face it, as annoying as the babe might be, she needs our help.

Booker decides that confronting Simone might not be the best course of action. "She's a bit moody since all this went down. Ya know, I get that some people say that time heals all and stuff, but that's not the case with this one." All I can think of is how this reality show will be the best on record, ever!

"We have only one real choice," Shea adds. "And that's to go back using the portal and retrieve her long-lost love." As soon as he gets the words out of his mouth, we realize that the next huge obstacle will be to decide who is going to do the dirty work. Who is going to make the round trip of their lives? Obviously, there are way too many risks to count. "Okay, okay. Let's grab some paper and write all this down," Shea says.

Matt scoops up the complimentary pen and pad, which are conveniently provided by the hotel. "Goals and obstacles list. Let's begin. First, get Thomas back over here. Second, avoid Lafitte. Third, we all survive. Pretty simple, I think."

Booker seems to be analyzing everything before it becomes fairly obvious that he has already thought about some of this prior to our recent pow-wow. He offers up additional info by informing us that a few lucky souls have made this infamous trip over the years. Even better, Booker makes us privy to the fact that some on the other side know the portal exists. Evidently, this is the main reason why the mystical source of transportation continues to change its home base. We soak up every word. Our ageless friend takes a decided pause before adding, "Lafitte himself has been looking for a way to come over here for years. Man, he has a long-lost treasure to collect."

Matt

Shea is mesmerized by the tale before he quizzes Booker about where the portal is located on the other side. "It changes," Booker says, "but it's always around the same place. Before you shoot me another question, I'll take it one step further. No, not anyone and everyone has been able to use it. That's why when all you arrived in this town, we all knew it was gonna be time for something to go down."

"The pictures," Shea asks. "What about all the photos, which date back so many years and are hung in the hallways?" Booker even had an answer for that. Evelyne pushed him forward about one hundred years, and it was a done deal.

As exciting as all this may sound, part of me is beginning to understand how scary it must have been and the overwhelming emptiness that Booker must have felt. He had no real sense of security. As annoying as brothers can be, there is still a constant reassurance that we have one another and a never-ending unconditional bond. However, I forbid myself from getting too sappy or emotional. After all, Andrew did swipe my last two iTunes cards without telling me.

"I've gone back a few times but never stayed for long," Booker informs us. "Sometimes, I think I won't be able to make it back over to this side. Once I realized, that, yeah, I can do a bit of time travelin', I could dig it."

Booker goes on to explain that the past is the same as it was the day he left, with all the situations remaining the same, including the dangers. The one thing that I can't seem to overlook is the real possibility of passing random people on the streets who might hail from entirely different centuries. This takes the notion of respecting one's elders to a whole new level.

Shea and Flynn can't stop asking Booker about what it was like during that last stormy night, when all hell broke loose. It seems there was an actual breaking point. Booker describes a scene of circus-like proportions. Everyone knew they were being forced out of their comfortable little home sites and thrust back into a world of uncertainties. Suddenly, Jean Lafitte's assurances and future dreams promising extreme wealth for everyone were being thrown out to sea, literally.

"Just who was this Thomas character?" Shea asks. "What exactly happened to him?"

Booker still seems transfixed by the evening in question so long ago. He appears to be going in and out of consciousness while speaking as if he is lying on a therapist's couch. "Thomas was an alright guy, I suppose. He had been wanting to get free from Lafitte for a while.

Jeal's schemes and promises were becoming nothing but a bunch of false hopes."

Andrew

I think we all know that Shea will soon become the token sacrifice. The only real surprise is when Flynn jumps up and down, exclaiming, "I'm so gonna step back in time. Instead of a step back on the court, I'm steppin' back in time for the sake of true love. I'm so stoked. Shea, dude, this is epic." If only the rest of us shared Flynn's unbridled enthusiasm and fearlessness. I may be only thirteen years old, but even I understand the risks.

Flynn continues his self-appointed pep rally while the rest of us, including Booker, ignore him and attempt to finalize every detail. We conclude that the upcoming departure will be the simplest aspect of our plan, a small concern. What if Shea and Flynn pop up in Lafitte's master bedroom? I can't imagine that would be a good thing. No guarantees here. Upon arrival, the hope is that Thomas won't be too difficult to locate. He was Jeal's right-hand man, after all. The warped thing about all this portal travel is the characters involved. I can't seem to find a vanilla one in the bunch. Some souls have been stuck in their own version of Groundhog Day, while others seem to be acutely aware of an alternative reality. Obviously, the crazy pirate is well aware that a fortune is awaiting him somewhere on the other side. To sum it all up, the man isn't happy. Grudges, after all.

Nonetheless, we are united and committed to our plan. The good thing is that none of us will tolerate defeat. A couple of days ago, we were solely focused on the teams in our tournament bracket, but now the only name on our lips is Jean Lafitte. Talk about complicated. This story has more layers than *Narcos*. Let's see, you have an angry crook who believes in magic and wants his stolen treasure returned.

Toss in a trusted employee who believed he could double-cross a real-life Lord Voldemort. What was he thinking? Oh, and let's not forget the epitome of the Mean Girl herself, Simone. Then there at those who only wanted to escape their current unfortunate trappings in life. Personally, I can't help but believe that Booker had some sort of futuristic insight into how he just couldn't miss a single decade of incredible NBA.

More power to them all.

‡Assist

Shea

For the first time in my fairly normal life, I am officially frightened. It's one thing to feel overwhelmed or even nervous before taking a geometry test or playing a top-ranked team. It's an entirely different sensation trying to wrap your head around the possibility of being permanently trapped inside a different world, without friends and family. Why am I doing this? Nonetheless, the plan is officially in motion and about to begin.

Flynn gathers his hoodie along with a drink and a protein bar. I suppose he feels that one last nutritional boost will help reassure his safety. I just want to make a final trip to the bathroom to throw up. What do I wear before entering such a bizarre type of combat? I can't seem to decide between the All-American Polo look or a more comfortable choice of attire, which includes my usual workout clothes. I opt for the latter. I might need additional ease of movement while making an escape. I run some shaping gel through my hair. I'm beginning to feel like I'm searching for any excuse to stall the inevitable.

As I take one last look in the mirror, I hear distinct rapping sounds from the other side of the door. "Shea, man, show time. Let's do your fade away and get this show on the road," Flynn says excitedly.

Now, I understand the importance of having my man Flynn on this mission. If nothing else, he will keep me calm because of his never-ending belief that we will come out on top. There is some truth to the meaning of "teamwork," after all. Slowly, I open the door. When I emerge, I make certain not to reveal the trepidation that is consuming me. Andrew has decided to be our wingman down at the bathroom stall, while Matt has given himself the cushy position of backup, hiding out inside our hotel room. Never one to feel as if he is in slacking, Matt reminds us how important his job is. He must make sure his cell phone is charged at all times and available to everyone. I'm trying to figure out if he's expecting a life-and-death Snapchat coming his way if we find ourselves expected to walk the plank. Oh well. At some point, I know we all must trust one another if we expect any of this to work.

Booker heads out toward the elevators. Andrew still insists on pushing the "down" button. I laugh to myself. Here we are in a rather intense situation, but in my thirteen-year-old brother's mind, that button still holds some importance. After the elevator doors close, we shift our focus to the lights that indicate which floor we are passing. Finally, the light holds steady. We have arrived. Booker makes a beeline straight for the lobby restroom. Maybe he will make a wrong turn. Wishful thinking.

Once again, we all gather in the stall. Booker makes sure no one else is present and then secures the lock. I guess that is the least we can do, prevent unsuspecting souls from being sucked down into a toilet filled with fake blue water and ending up who knows where. Please, let the toilets be clean.

"Well, now what?" I ask Booker. We are standing by a ceramic bowl and looking inside it while expecting something to magically occur.

"I know, I know. Sometimes, it can be a little bit tricky. Both you brothers just stand right here." He positions Flynn and me to where our feet are just touching the base of the bathroom fixture. "Look down, and don't divert your eyes. Not even once," Booker whispers. He makes his way to the entrance of the room and turns off the lights. How are we supposed to keep our focus inside a toilet if we can't even see it?

I detect Booker making his way back over to where we are standing, and he gives us a final reassuring hug. Alas, the familiar flushing noises begin. They seem to go on indefinitely. Flushing and more flushing and still more flushing. I'm beginning to doubt that anything is going to happen, but then it does. I feel a huge gush of wind followed by an intense force on my body. My head whips around, and my feet are no longer touching the ground. At this point, I can't hold my eyes open, and I feel a huge spinning sensation. I have flashbacks to carnival rides from years ago. My body seems like it's glued to an imaginary Velcro wall, and the floor keeps dropping.

I'm not sure how long my supernatural ride actually lasts. It's probably best that it is all a complete blur. The one thing I can recall is how I remained completely dry up until right now. I'm soaking wet! Boom! Flynn arrives. We are both sitting inside a water trough, surrounded by a bunch of animals who appear rather thirsty. This experience gives an entirely different meaning to the term "spin cycle."

Andrew

The event lasted no more than a minute, max. In fact, it took less time than my last few free throws during overtime. I'm unable to move and am beginning to doubt if I'm even breathing. It may be pitch dark, but the sensation currently filling the bathroom is unlike any I have ever experienced. An uncomfortable hollowness fills me. It reminds me of when I downed a two-liter Dr. Pepper on an empty stomach. Booker turns the lights back on, and I immediately ask, "Now what?"

Booker describes this next part of the puzzle as being the most difficult. "We just have to wait it out."

As Booker and I re-enter our room, Matt peppers us with all kinds of questions. After about the fifth inquiry, Booker holds his hands up for Matt to stop. Matt isn't the least bit deterred. "I'm dying here. Help a guy out!" The three of us sit down by the window. The craziness of what has just occurred downstairs seems oddly out of place as we watch tourists outside relaxing. Couples walk hand in hand, mindlessly meandering down pathways. Instead of any unsettling sounds of potential distress, the only things any of us hear are partiers from below. I'm certain their biggest worry is applying some aloe vera later because of too much sun.

Matt interrupts our surreal moment. "You know, I hate to point out the obvious, but we don't have all the time in the world. Just how long do you think any of us can really carry on this little charade in front of our parents? Not to mention the fact we're supposed to be here and actually show up at some basketball games. Are we just supposed to ask some 'not alive' guys to suit up and take our place?"

It is the first time that I can see the nerves and tension truly beginning to consume us. I also detect the gradual seeping in of anger. I know my brother. Matt is not about to sit around and allow something awful to happen to Shea or Flynn, for that matter.

Booker must be reading Matt's thoughts, because he decides to interject some of his 150 years of wisdom. "For whatever reason, your arrival has set all these wheels in motion. I believe in some of that way-out stuff, man. I've seen things. I know—or knew—Evelyne. I know she made sure to protect us when she cast some of her spells. I swear that all this must have been predestined from the onset. I really believe that! Bottom line is that you just have to have faith."

The three of us sit still for a moment before I nod my head. Matt and I remind Booker that our top priority is the safety of our friend and brother, but we would love to have somewhat of a time frame. Booker finally cracks a smile. "Don't you two know by now that the mental game is just as important as your shot?"

✦ Screen

Matt

As we wait and wait and wait some more, I get flashbacks of much more relaxing family togetherness. My mind drifts off to eating a hot dog at Yankee stadium, going to Port A and getting golf carts stuck in the sand, and riding Universal Studio rides so many times that I got sick. Good times. None of those activities have fully prepared me for the drama of long-lost treasures or ghosts. How I can't wait to be at home with a juicy Chick-Fil-A sandwich in my hands. I anticipated this tournament being tough, but I had no idea it was going to end up like this. I'm beginning to feel guilty about not insisting I go through portal or even sending Shea with an additional cell phone. I wonder if it's possible to connect with a different time period. The data usage is bound to be expensive. I'd hate to see that month's bill. Either way, I want to do something more to help than just play the waiting game.

Andrew remains sprawled out playing on his phone. Booker is furiously texting away. I dare not interrupt him. I don't have to worry about figuring out what my friend is busy doing anymore when he startles us and leaps to his feet. "Let's go. I made some arrangements down at the Strand. There are some hotel bikes we can use out front. Now."

Doesn't this guy have a car? I have to remind myself that it is highly doubtful that Booker even has a valid driver's license. I don't remember the last time I rode a bike for actual transportation, but I'll give it a go. I'm not usually someone who is game for doing anything dangerous. Heck, I won't even watch a horror movie after dark. However, on this particular evening, coupled with the circumstances surrounding us, I don't give the task a second thought. I feel worthless knowing that my brother and Flynn are risking their lives for some girl that they don't even know.

Andrew, Booker, and I make our way outside and locate a small bike rack tucked behind some hedges. These wheels might not be the latest in road bike style, but the tires are all pumped up. Somehow, I'm pretty sure we are not taking a late-night trip to get some ice cream. Turns out I am correct in my assumption, because Booker informs us that our destination is none other than some creepy witchcraft shop, after hours, no less. Cars stream by, but we keep our eye on the prize, the other side of the island.

Being with a local has its advantages. If anyone knows their way around the beach strip, it's Booker. As we pedal away, it becomes apparent that the years haven't damaged Booker in the fitness department. It's a shame that we can't use him on our team. He claims he spends all his time off shooting buckets, and I don't doubt it. He's ripped. I think the age-limit rules might prove to be an obstacle though. Booker's birth certificate is bound to raise questions.

Luckily, the Strand isn't too far away, and after about ten minutes, we are smack dab in the middle of all the hustle and bustle. The stores are beginning to close down, but tourists are still lingering everywhere. Booker instructs us to leave our bikes, and we begin our trek to the land of hocus pocus. It is unnerving to think that my trusted companion has the local witch on speed dial. Oh well, at this point, I just go with the flow.

As we pass all sorts of quaint storefronts, one in particular causes Andrew to stop dead in his tracks. "The candy shop! Please, Matt?" This must be when years of wisdom become so helpful. Booker quickly diffuses the situation by promising Andrew a private, personal, belated visit, complete with extra sugar, if he can wait. I can't help but wonder if this poor shop has any idea what is about to hit them.

Booker makes one last turn before stopping in front of a discreet wooden sign dangling precariously out front with the help of some turn-of-the-century rods. The writing on the window promises customers the opportunity to find true love, prosperity, and inner peace. Do they ensure tournament wins too? Instead of entering through the front door, we follow Booker down the back alley, where he stops outside the employee entrance. He knocks three times and then places his hands inside his pockets.

"Oh well, they aren't here," Andrew says. "Let's go back for the candy."

As soon as the words are out of his mouth, a middle-aged black woman opens the door. She evokes a warm, gracious greeting before reaching out for Booker. "Baby, it's been way too long. Why don't you come visit more often? I'll even make your favorite stuffed shrimp if you'll just come around."

Booker follows the woman inside, almost forgetting he has arrived with visitors. Andrew and I file in behind him.

The talkative lady continues her conversation with Booker while motioning for us to take a seat. The living room is filled with several purple settees and small ornate lamps. The vibe reminds me of my visit to the French Quarter because of all the color and vivid artwork adorning the walls.

After a few more minutes of eavesdropping on their small talk, which includes bits and pieces of basketball, Booker redirects the conversation back to the real reason for our late-night visit. "Introductions first, Miss Eva. These guys are staying at the Galvez. I 'member you saying that Daniel is playing in that tournament. That's what brought these guys to town."

Eva smiles and then spends the next few minutes offering us refreshments and silently sizing us up. I must say, her red velvet cake is the best I've ever eaten. Andrew even asks for seconds. We soon discover that we are playing in an annual tournament that grows bigger every year. I doubt Miss Eva has ever met a stranger. Wouldn't you know it, just as I'm getting even more comfortable, our conversation turns south down a serious detour. Booker sets down his bottle of old-fashioned Coke and looks directly at Eva. "Things are happening, and I'm afraid this time may be different. A couple of guys went down the portal. I mean, like, they're on the other side as we speak. If that isn't enough, Simone is getting totally out of control. I swear, Miss E., I'm beginning to feel some strange things deep inside me. We need your help."

Eva listens quietly and then makes her way closer to where Andrew is sitting and strokes his hair. This might be one of the few times I have ever seen my little brother remain still. "I bet you're a pretty good little point guard." Eva doesn't seem to expect a reply.

She moves toward a bookcase, which is blocking an unused hallway. She pulls a couple of books off the shelf before plopping down on one of the velvet sofas. Page after page, the sound of paper turning is the only thing resonating in the room. Eventually, her fingers stop, landing on one particular passage. Eva reaches for her reading glasses, which have been dangling around her neck, and slides them up her nose. We all wait for her to finish, unsure of what will be determined from this impromptu home school session.

After five minutes pass, we are startled when Eva slams the book shut and gathers us before her. She places a white candle in the middle of a round table. "The way I see it, the spell that should work the best offers protection from outside negatives only if everyone can unite together as a real team. Your courage and loyalty to each other must be felt deep inside your hearts."

Booker appears deep in thought. "What if we aren't even sure what harm is being thrown our way? I mean, who's doing the honors?"

Eva provides no answer. Instead, her attention is solely on her upcoming spell. I had assumed we would be privy to one of the different colored potions inside one of the many old-looking bottles that are strewn all over the shelves. Everywhere I look inside the store is nothing but containers promising to improve lives. I assume those trinkets are mostly for cruise ship passengers, who fill the streets every afternoon. I believe we are about to partake in the real deal.

Eva carefully screws a blue lightbulb inside a tiny crystal lamp while reaching for a sprig of herbs. I don't even begin to ask what is inside the twine, but I'm sure it matters to her. The lights are dim, and a soft, blue haze comes from the lamp. Eva closes her eyes while dropping her hands to her sides, indicating we are to do the same. Andrew has the sweatiest palms I have ever felt in my life. However, now is probably not the best time to grab a towel.

Eva pulls a small silver chain out from beneath her blouse, displaying it in full view. I conclude that the symbol sliding along the links is a mystic star. I'm betting Eva isn't big on modern technology.

"In this place and this hour, guard us. Take the keys to our hearts, and close the doors of our minds to evil doings"

The simple phrases spoken from the local witch last only a few seconds. She squeezes our hands tightly. I sneak a peek and see her open her eyes as she blows out the candle. It is about then that I realize that I have not heard a sound from Booker. He is still sitting in a zombie-like state, looking at the floor. Then he screams at the top of his lungs! We all freeze, unsure what to make of it. As if it was no big deal, Booker gets out of his chair and pushes it under the table. "Cool, Miss E. You're the best!"

Booker gives our hostess one last kiss on the cheek and promises to meet up with her during one of the games. Strangely, he acts like this is almost a normal occurrence. Maybe he has done this once or twice before.

Shea *(On the Other Side)*

A water trough! Seriously! All I can think about is the backwash. I'm looking directly into the eyes of three pigs, who each have runny noses. Next up, I see a lone donkey, who isn't pleased to find a couple of soaking-wet humans splashing around in front of him. I've always heard about donkeys and their tempers. You don't have to tell me twice. Flynn decides to play nice with the natives and attempts to cozy up to the resident Hogzilla. I have to shake him back to reality. I look at our endeavor as if it's a serious chess game. I need to keep planning a couple of moves ahead. We must remember the exact location of the disgusting pig pen.

We escape the confines of the rickety container, and I wring the excess water from the bottom of my shirt. As I look around, I realize how bad the visibility is because of the weather. My thoughts are interrupted by several loud sounds emerging all around us. It doesn't take any longer to remind us that we have entered one of the most storied sagas from local folklore. Families are desperately gathering up all their belongings, and the sounds of confused children crying are everywhere. I detect some shouting coming from directly in front of where we are standing and decide that the best course of action might be to go where there is the least amount of activity, Lafitte's Red House.

Flynn and I do our best to locate the beachfront. Both of us remember seeing the remains of what is left of the pirate's old home as we drove into the city. I wonder if Lafitte has caught wind of the fact that his once-stately manor is now just an enclosed area with a bronze plaque standing in front of a cheap aluminum fence. At the moment, the man's crib is the nicest place around and faces his own personal ocean of lawlessness. "Flynn, follow the lights. Look over there. Notice how things seem more orderly, calm almost." Despite our out-of-place attire, I'm not really worried that we will be noticed. Everyone is in full-blown survival mode right out of a scene from the latest Transformers movie. Off we go.

"Shea, I kind of feel bad. I mean, it's not fair. Can we try bringing the donkey across?"

Ugh!

The good news is that all our workouts seem to have prepared us for making it up to the infamous building without becoming too winded.

Suddenly, Flynn motions me to stop. "Duck!"

The front door opens, and a few burly men welcome a large black woman, who is wearing the most colorful satin scarf I have ever seen. I can think of a few girls I know who would kill to wear that hair accessory the next time they hit the beach.

Flynn and I sidestep our way to the back of the house, making sure we go unnoticed. We see a small window and decide that our best bet to see what's going on inside is to scale the wall. After a few minor wrestling moves, we are positioned to catch our first real glimpse into the night that was.

Inside is a slave, a good-looking twenty-something man, the large woman, and Lafitte himself. Flynn and I are transfixed. Still, we know what we have come to do. We need to bring Thomas back over with us while not alerting Jean Lafitte.

Lafitte appears to have been the stud of the day. When he stands upright, he is taller than I expected. I can tell that he likes to dress, simply by looking at his threads. Compared to the other men in the room, the pirate's flair for adornment makes him stand out. As I size him up, my heart skips a few beats when his attention seems drawn to the window. I'm sure he must feel our presence, but then he swings back around while addressing the younger man. "Thomas," he says in a low, confident voice. "I'm putting you in charge of the most important event of the night. I have complete trust in you. Understand?"

Thomas looks him directly in the eyes before replying. "Yes, sir. You can count on me."

Checkmate.

Thomas

Simone. I imagine the definition of "perfection" was penned to describe her. I remember the first time I saw her long golden hair. She was tall and graceful and seemed to float around as if her feet never touched the floor. Simply put, she was stunning. I'm certain Simone could have had anyone she wanted, but for some strange reason, she chose me. There are still days I pinch myself, because I feel like I might wake up from this dream, and she will vanish. I'm certain that my over-the-top love-struck rhetoric may sound a bit old fashioned, but this is the era I'm from. Unfortunately, I'm stuck in a long-lost world, and she is forever a ghost.

How I wish I could rewrite our last evening together. I would have done so many things differently. If I had known what Lafitte was capable of, I would have gladly thrown away my silly desires for wealth in exchange for a chance to live happily ever after with Simone. The tears I have since cried could easily have filled an ocean by now, or at least Lake Austin. One catchphrase that seems to never go out of style is, "Hindsight is 20/20." Now I'm forced to relive my self-inflicted tragic events over and over, praying that, one of these days, something will change our inevitable course.

When news came to me that Simone had thrown herself off the hotel roof, I died myself. Well, I didn't physically die, but I might as well have. Leave it to Simone to garner headlines. I must admit, despite her huge heart, her contagious giggles, and her extreme hotness (I learned this phrase from a few visitors), she could be difficult to handle. Perhaps that is why she was a perfect fit for me. Simone was always able to keep me on my toes.

So many decades have passed since the night that everything ended for me. I was always taught that time heals all wounds. Ha! That's not true. I'm stuck in the past as if it's a mandatory prison sentence. I would have much preferred walking the plank. Sometimes, I hear a few rumblings about how Simone continues roaming up and down the corridors of the big hotel, looking for me and my ship. Initially, I'm sure she would give me some grief if we ever did reunite, but maybe there's still a chance. Some nights, I lie awake in a cold sweat worried that my bride to be has already hooked up with someone else. Simone was quite the flirt. I choose to remain confident that true love is unbreakable.

I have never been a true believer in voodoo or even superstitions, for that matter. Madame Evelyne was probably the first person Lafitte brought with him to the island when he left New Orleans. I feel pretty confident in saying that Lafitte places more importance on her than he even has on his prized ships. She was essentially given to him as a sort of parting gift from the queen herself, Marie Leveau. It was common knowledge that Lafitte was quite the regular in the French Quarter. He never even thought about devising any of his plots without assistance from what he believed to be supernatural powers.

Evelyne enters the parlor and assesses who is present. She raises her arms and throws back her head. As always, she is theatrical. Her dress is quite voluminous and sweeps the floor, a few pieces of black lace peeking out from beneath her petticoats. She doesn't wear much makeup, with the exception of bright red lipstick.

She makes some humming noises, every once in a while interjecting a low-grade grunt. We have experienced similar demonstrations before and recognize when we are expected to take a seat. Tonight's spell is to ensure Lafitte's safety and maintain his prosperity. Been there, done that. Evelyne motions for Lafitte to sit, and she shoves a couple of handheld mirrors in his face. The man doesn't flinch. All I can think about is how there is no other soul around who can boss the Boss around like she does.

"Close eyes." We all follow her cues. After experiencing this deja vu moment so many times before, even Evelyne tweaks her spells a time or two. A white candle is burning in the center of the room. The woman begins brushing the lead pirate's hair forward into his face. "Think of what you desire," she whispers. Then she begins counting, and her voice slowly increases in volume after every phrase. "Look in the mirror. LOOK IN THE MIRROR!" Lafitte grabs the reflective device and appears to be in a trance. The priestess turns toward us, signaling us to remain where we are.

It appears there are still more tricks in the woman's bag. Evelyne pulls out a small container, into which she blows an air kiss before raising it toward the moon. Once again, her every move seems to be exaggerated. She begins dispensing a thick clumpy oil all over the wooden floor. Until now, I was kind of enjoying this dog and pony show. Unfortunately, I have a sick sense that we are about to undergo a good old-fashioned spring cleaning and be forced to scrub down the floors.

"Rain!" Evelyne continues.

"You heard the woman! Get your sorry butts outside and gather up some water!" Lafitte says. I guess he comprehends these spells much better than the rest of us.

Out the door we go. We are gone no more than a few minutes before returning with a couple of half-full buckets of fresh rainwater. Evelyne seems impressed with our efficiency. She tears off portions of her ill-fitted undergarments, and the slave instantly kneels and begins scrubbing away. Good workers are hard to find, what with Booker and Caesar gone now. Evelyne seems to have calmed down somewhat, and she proceeds to blow out the candle. She reaches down for her infamous satchel while making her way over to Lafitte one last time.

"The oil bring luck." Her hands gently brush his cheeks. I have a feeling that even Lafitte's latest paramour wasn't this intimate with him.

I decide to help out with the clean-up duty. None of us say a word. I'm lost in my thoughts, but I could swear I just heard something outside the window.

Time is of the essence. My heart is pounding, and I feel myself beginning to sweat uncontrollably. Once again, like time and time before, I have carefully tucked away all the doubloons deep inside my distressed leather satchel. I'm never quite sure where my next source of nourishment will come from. So, I have gathered loaves of bread and some fresh fruit, which is lying on top of the priceless goods. As if that weren't enough, I have taken extra precautions and helped myself to some of Jean's personal stash of expensive rums. I just might need them for quenching my thirst. Everyone is far too busy to notice that I have been given strict instructions from the man himself. However, I'm forging ahead with another plan. I must leave immediately to have a chance to escape and ensure a future for Simone and me.

My hands can't even feel the slick doorknob as I reach for it and turn the handle. All I want is to land safely on the other side. While I admit I have some type of warped respect for Lafitte's genius and physical abilities, I'm astutely aware that he is getting up in years. I have been privy to all the secret meetings between the slaves, the crew, and even the village. Lafitte has worn out their trust and, more importantly, betrayed their loyalties. I, on the other hand, just want my freedom and my girl.

The heavy door finally opens. I try not to slam it as I leave. Everything I need is with me, and I pick up the pace. I see my waiting ship just one hundred yards away, and I can almost taste everything I have worked so hard for.

Boom!

The right side of my body is engulfed by a massive force, followed by my sudden introduction to the cold, wet ground. I feel the weight of a larger body lying on top of me, preventing me from getting up. The wind has been knocked out of me, and my head is pulsing. I want to reach up and grab the top of my hair to ensure I'm still alive. God, it hurts!

"Don't say a word! Nothing!" Those are the only words I hear. I don't think these strangers have to worry about me uttering anything. I'm useless.

I feel another set of arms reach beneath me and scoop me up. My manliness is now in serious question. I'm glad my woman isn't witnessing any of this. Talk about embarrassing.

The different voices let me know I'm being carried away from the craziness of the Red House. Lafitte's current abode slowly gives way to the earthier sounds of a much more remote area. I feel my chest rising and falling in a somewhat steady breathing pattern.

"Look at us," a voice whispers. I don't recognize its origins. As frightened as I am, I'm also curious as to who my kidnappers are. I clench my fists and then open my eyes. I'm staring up into rainy skies and am surrounded by a bunch of smelly livestock. I look all around, only to be caught by surprise when two foreigners jump above me.

"Thomas," the young men say in unison. It's dark, and I can't make out their unique clothing. One of the men maintains his tight grip on me, which prevents me from making a getaway. "I know you have no idea who we are. The problem is, there's no time to explain. You will just have to follow us."

A pounding headache sets in. Let's see, I can trust these strangers or continue my never-ending quest for the ship while also trying to outmaneuver one of the sneakiest crooks ever to live. As I'm making up my mind, the owner of the large hands adds, "Simone needs you." That settles it.

Andrew

Man, that was some crazy stuff back there. I don't even know if I'm going to be up to doing the whole dress-up thing at Halloween this year. We all say our goodbyes, and I'm secretly hoping that Ms. E. will text me her cake recipe.

The bike ride back to the hotel seems a bit longer, but it might be because none of us are speaking, and everything seems a bit more intense. Either that or it's the extra slice of cake weighing heavily on my gut. After about ten minutes, I spot the hotel's lights looming in the distance. As creepy as the fortress has become to me, it still feels safer than the little shop of horrors we just left. I don't think I will even mind the spaced-out mystery girl roaming the halls.

Booker has us park our bikes in the front, and we all head up to the crib. I wonder if these guys even have tomorrow's game on their radar anymore. I don't want to be the bearer of bad news, but the team they'll be playing will most likely have slept. Leaving for this sleepy, little coastal town seems like a distant memory. At this point, we are forced to sit and wait for the official return of Shea and Flynn. Perhaps they will arrive with an additional passenger.

Matt grabs the remote and searches for a playoff game. He is quite the multi-tasker. His right hand firmly clutches the TV controller while his left hand simultaneously searches for his phone. Evidently, it doesn't matter in what year you originate; modern times have officially consumed us all. Booker is also scrolling through his numerous Instagram accounts and responding to texts. Okay, twist my arm. I suppose I will follow suit. My problem is, I can't seem to keep my mind focused on junior high drama. How I wish I could just revert back into my former little world. I decide to partake in some online research of my own and look up Galveston ghosts. Simone has made the cut. Evidently, she is quite the celebrity in this realm, because ghost hunters continue visiting this place in hopes of catching even a brief glimpse of her. No wonder she's delivering Oscar-worthy performances all the time. Theater and all. I understand her better after reading some of this stuff.

Suddenly, the three of us are shaken out of our silence by a strong jolt and a strange, sharp sound. The eeriness of the moment causes me to drop my phone. They're on their way back.

Shea

We have him! We have Thomas! Before the poor love-struck guy can change his mind, we all jump inside the mildew-smelling water trough. These people really owe it to these animals to clean these things out once in a while. Note to self: I will return home and be much more diligent when feeding my dog every morning. I have yet to release my tight grip on this unsuspecting soul. Flynn and I have manned him up, but sometimes a person's adrenaline can enable him to lift a small car. We aren't taking any chances.

The one thing we are not prepared for is our trip home. The toilet was kind of a no brainer, in that a toilet has few functions. All you can do is flush it. It never occurred to me to ask how to use the trough to get back. "Well, how do we begin?" I ask, keeping my hold on Thomas. Flynn sits still, but I can tell he is genuinely thinking things through.

"The animals. Let's try and get them to come drink." The plan sounds ridiculous, but it also seems plausible. After all, the purpose of a water trough is to give water to the animals. Good enough for me.

I reach for the protein bars. Flynn grabs some of the makeshift bait, and the three of us quietly entice the barnyard menagerie toward us. All it takes is one of the critters to take a bite before the rest will follow suit. The drinking concept is sure to follow. First up, the precocious donkey. I swear the four-legged creature really does think he's smarter than us. He ambles toward us, and Thomas tosses a few pieces to the unsuspecting animal. He likes it! Thank goodness!

The next thing I know, the three of us are sitting in the middle of the worn-out structure, which feels as if it might collapse at any second, enveloped by thirsty animals. They don't let up for a second when it comes to their insatiable need for water. Slowly but surely, the water's movements form into small cyclones. The force becomes greater and greater, never easing up. Ironically, this activity gives me flashbacks to my younger years when we would run in one direction inside a packed hot tub. The only difference here is that our current experience is probably life or death. "Keep drinking. Don't stop." I reach for another piece of the soaked peanut butter-flavored bar and offer it up. If these animals are anything like my dog, they'll keep chowing down. Sure enough, the plan seems to be working.

Despite the continuous downpour, Flynn, Thomas, and I are able to grab hands and maintain eye contact. Moments later, the eerie sensation duplicates the feelings from our flight over here. Everything rushes back to me like a bad dream. I feel the pulling and the force and the unmistakable hollow tunnel sensation. The moonlit night is gray, and low-grade howling noises soon follow. How I can't wait for this journey to end.

Bam! Unlike our trip to the Red House, our landing is horribly unsteady and even a bit painful. I open my eyes, only to discover the cause of my soon-to-be black and blues. We are on piled on top of each other on the restroom's cold tiled floor, complete with a don-key's foot wedged into my back. Really? I suppose Flynn got his wish after all. I mean, who wouldn't want to help a donkey escape the grips of an infamous pirate? Flynn must be feeling my pain, because he is already attempting to put a positive spin on our situation. "Shea, man, it was meant to be. We'll just suit him up and get him upstairs." Then he turns his attention to the donkey, stroking his mane as if he was a newborn baby.

Thomas and I stand up and dust ourselves off. Unlike before, I'm no longer the recent transplant. The man straightens himself up as he sighs and asks the obvious. "Now what?"

Before I can answer him, the door opens to reveal the one soul at this hotel who can maybe relate to our new misfit: Booker. He stum-bles in and then locks the door. (I hope that not too many people are going to be in need of this particular restroom tonight.)

"You scrubs. I could hear your rear ends all the way up on the fifth floor!" Thomas recognizes a familiar voice and turns around to go in for some serious bromance. His arms are extended in front of him, and he looks as if he might cry. Booker gives him a huge smile. "I got 'em proposin' just like they do on the court." The two old friends share an extended hug before Booker finally pushes Thomas off. "Yo, man, not too much of that now." Thomas laughs and for the first time tonight seems to be at ease.

After winding things down, we reconvene back in the room. Flynn reminds us that the donkey will most likely need some assistance. Never one to be without some creative resources up his sleeve, or hoodie, Booker figures out a way to hide the furry pet using the cargo elevator. All in all, Mr. Ed Jr. seems pretty laid back. Up the elevator we go. I figure he's the least of our worries.

As I look back on this entire evening, it is a shame that none of us ever noticed that Lafitte watched us depart and will soon be on his way...

⁞ Double Dribble

Andrew

They made it back safely. Thank goodness. I'm eager to meet the new guy and can't wait to talk to Shea and Flynn. The thing is, major events seem to call for even more major calories. After a quick phone call to the lobby restaurant, I'm chosen as the token waiter for the evening.

They tell me all I have to do is slide over to the bar and grab the waiting tray. Booker's employment definitely has its advantages. I know from experience how much the little extras can add up on the final tally. Trust me, I have been on the receiving end of the bill as my mom checks out of one of these places. It isn't good.

With my phone in hand, I'm not feeling even a tiny bit nervous. I maneuver next to some guy who obviously feels the need for one more drink before his night comes to an end. The other thirsty customers never give me a second glance, but the bartender realizes who I am. He smiles and adds even more bags of gourmet chips and chicken wings to my platter. Shea will be thrilled! How are we expected to concentrate on such serious matters without proper nourishment? Unlike Booker, the bartender is much older and more polished, in an old-school kind of way. He is perfectly dressed, his bowtie in place.

"Do I need to sign anything?" I ask. The man shakes his head, so I make my way to a waiting elevator. Using my elbow, I hit the button for the fifth floor and wait for the doors to shut. I can smell the comforting aroma of warm brie and hear the open coke bottles fizzing away. Yum!

The doors are almost shut, and I'm beyond eager to sit down in front of a good old-fashioned Disney movie while stuffing my face with the items I'm holding. That's when I notice a figure approaching. I don't really pay it much attention. Big mistake! Once he stands directly in front of me, he looks all too familiar. His appearance is followed by a haunting voice that causes me to forget every thought that was recently in my head. "That sure is a lot of food for a little guy like you." With that, the doors slam shut.

Crash! The tray hits the elevator floor, and I can't even begin to start gathering up the mess. I see the floor numbers increasing as I search frantically for my phone. I believe this may be the first time I have ever truly felt claustrophobic.

"What?" Matt's says after answering. I speak a mile a minute while making no sense. No matter. My rambling must have been enough to convince everyone that something was up, because I hear footsteps running outside the elevator doors.

I attempt to scoop up all the dirty food morsels. Actually, the scene in front of me looks similar to something my dog threw up recently. The doors open, and the entire squad is here. "Forget all this. Let's just get back to the room," Booker mumbles. We do as we are told.

After a few details of my play by play, I get to the main event. "The door was shutting, and there he was, Lafitte!" How no one could have been aware of an impending visit from a notorious pirate is beyond me. I would think that if one of us was going to make a return trip back to a day where they might be rubbing shoulders with one of the cruelest crooks of all time, I don't know, maybe pay attention. None of us is certain when the Brad Pitt wannabe showed up to the modern day, but alas, he made a safe flight.

Booker gets up and faces the window again while the others continue talking over one another. Thomas remains silent. I remind myself how far back Thomas and Booker go. I would have to classify their friendship as seriously long-term. Booker faces us before answering. "This might change a few things, but it's nothing we can't handle."

"How can you even begin to say that?" Shea blurts. "A total psycho is walking around right now in our midst! He has killed people, and he's staying in our hotel. Oh, and let's not forget that he is specifically looking for us!" Always the seasoned gentleman, Thomas does his best to try and calm us down while also reassuring us that everything is going to be all right.

In the midst of the drama, our locked hotel door is blown off its hinges. The room goes dark, and our cell phones shut off. I can no longer see my hands in front of me. The temperature drops to a bone-tingling sub-zero. Despite the chill, a red flame erupts inside the room. It forms a circle around us, and something causes the furniture to sway from side to side. Every time I try to open my eyes wider, I feel a horrible burning sensation that forces me to close them again.

I reach for the bedframe, hoping not to get blown away because of the sheer force of it all. I'm going to classify all this as some serious strength training.

"When were you going to mention to me that you returned?" Of course, we should have been expecting Simone. She is now front and center.

Thomas

I should have anticipated the impending arrival of my girl, Simone. Truly, this is all my fault. She was always a girl who would find something out before having ever been told. In the modern world, Simone would most assuredly be someone who would know every password for her significant other's social media accounts. She never left any stone unturned. Oh well, despite all the time that has elapsed, she remains the most beautiful girl I have ever laid eyes on. Sure, she looks a bit transparent since the last time I saw her, and her hair might be in need of a trim, but she hasn't aged a bit.

Despite the presence of my newfound friends, it might as well be just me and Simone in the room. I get the impression that her visit is solely because of me. I'm flattered. It appears she has been unable to get me out of her system. Love does conquer all.

"Simone, you must try to calm down and stop all the dramatics. I've come here with the sole purpose of rejoining you. Not a day has gone by that my thoughts aren't filled with images of you, of us." I'm doing pretty well for myself until Flynn feels the need to chime in.

"Well, man, don't forget about the treasure thing and maybe trying to get out of Dodge." Simone reacts to this last statement by turning Flynn's cell phone into an inferno. She always did know how to hit someone where it hurts.

As Flynn tries to snuff out his phone, I approach Simone and embrace her. The only snag is that my arms go right through her. Somehow, she still manages to attach herself to my torso. Indeed, this must be a strange sight to witness. Her head is poking out from behind my right shoulder, and her legs are draped around my left side. Simone's head is lying on the nook of my neck as she showers me with kisses. I don't dare tell her that I can't feel them. After all, it's the thought that counts. Finally, Booker states that this is why he avoids her at all costs. I'm beginning to sense those two don't always see eye to eye.

"Get a room," Matt snipes at me.

Oh, sorry, we're already in a room. I do my best to soldier on with our plan while not upsetting Simone. Eventually, I have a thought. "It occurs to me that Jean is making a huge effort to prevent me from reconnecting with Simone. He may hold a grudge, but this mysterious Holy Grail he's seeking must be worth a lot!

Shea is obviously entertaining similar thoughts, and he faces Booker. No words are spoken, but suspicion seems to be building in the direction of our dear colleague. Might he know more than he's letting on? The celebratory mood shifts rapidly into an accusatory atmosphere.

"Are there any other reasons you wanted to bring Thomas over to this side?" Shea asks. It finally dawns on the former slave that he's on the hot seat. But Booker is saved by the bell. Simultaneously, all our phones begin buzzing with the reminder that it is now curfew. It looks like the question will have to be shelved for a later date. In the meantime, "Thomas, you get the floor tonight."

⁘ And One

Matt *(Day Four)* //

We are finishing up with our latest game, and it looks like we're advancing to the final four. Okay, it might not be the same as playing in the Big Dance, but it's always nice to make it to the final couple of rounds. I look around the gym and try anticipating which court we will be assigned to next. With only a few seconds left, my muscles are burning. Don't let anyone tell you that lactic acid isn't real. I would have to challenge them to hours of hoops. If my soreness from basketball isn't enough to push me over the edge, tedious ghost hunting will do it.

We make our way to the bench and gather our stuff. My mom comes over to where we're standing and blows me a kiss. She knows me too well. I enjoy seeing her excitement but don't necessarily want that fact to go public. Image, after all.

Now that our game is over, all I can think about is food. The car ride back to the hotel is pretty uneventful, and we acknowledge that we aren't able to stomach anything without first taking a fast shower. (It wouldn't be fair to the waitresses.)

As I make my way from the shower to the bedroom, I hear some cackling sounds from the movie playing on the TV and see Andrew and Dax hanging on every word. Wouldn't you know it, *Pirates of the Caribbean* is showing. There's Johnny Depp adorned with all the paraphernalia that any pirate worth their sea salt would want to wear. "Seriously, Andrew. Are you kidding me?"

Andrew glances up and reminds me that this trip is supposed to be a vacay for him. "At least change it to the playoffs during commercials," I respond. After all, what basketball player would ever think of missing a round-five game while visiting for a tournament, no less? Kids these days.

I try to spruce myself up without looking like I tried too hard. As I give my hair a last-minute finger comb, Andrew leaps to his feet. "KD or Steph? The Beard or the Mustache?" Oh, how I wish I could spend even a few minutes inside Andrew's head. The world is an unsettled mess right now, and his primary focus is on which player would frighten me the most.

"I don't know, Andrew. All of them would be pretty terrifying one on one." We pause for a moment before breaking into laughter. Actually, that felt kind of good. These past few days have been pretty intense. Our latest interruption was a much-needed release. I tell Andrew where I'm headed without trying to alarm Dax. I make my way over to Booker's secret enclave and see that the gang is all present. It becomes apparent that Booker is the man in charge.

"First up, nice moves today." His unexpected comment instantly helps break any existing tension and subtly reminds us that we are a team.

"How about Daniel?" I think we may end up playing him in the final. "Then what? Sit in the middle?" I ask sarcastically.

Booker chuckles. "Man, don't do me like that right now." We share a few more self-congratulatory remarks before winding the conversation down to the inevitable.

The tone turns decidedly serious, and Shea clears his throat as he sits up. "Booker, listen, before we go any further, we all have to know what the heck happened to whatever treasure was supposedly sent over. This isn't the time to avoid the elephant in the room. Dead serious. What do you really know about it?"

Our questioning snaps Thomas out of his comatose state. He seconds Shea's remarks, and then we all await Booker's impending response. It appears he anticipated our concerns. He doesn't show an ounce of hesitation as he looks prepared to be totally forthright with us. "Evelyne handed me some beat-up satchel that night. She literally swung the thing over my shoulders while she instructed me to jump inside some stinky water trough. You have to understand how crazy everything was that night. Ms. E. was offering me a chance for freedom. I didn't even give it a second thought when she told me to carry that worn-out thing."

I can tell that Booker is feeling some of the same emotions that he must have been feeling that awful night. As I look at him, I can only be grateful that I was not there. This kind of drama is the stuff that I have to read about in history class, but only when I'm really paying attention. For maybe the first time, it sinks in what some of those historical people might have been feeling when they lived through the pages of those books. There were faces behind their names, and each one had a personality, hopes, and feelings.

While I remain lost in thought, Shea is fully present in the here and now. "This still doesn't explain where the bag ended up once you arrived on this side. I don't get it. Did you just land here wet and take off running?"

Booker almost appears to be shrinking in size. Finally, he gathers the strength to detail what he remembers happening when he emerged inside the busy hotel kitchen. According to his best recollection, no one noticed him. He describes a kitchen filled with sparse vegetables and chickens running around. There were no James Beard award-winning chefs, that's for sure. The food was decadent for the day but only because of hard-working short-order cooks who knew how to throw together a great rack of lamb.

"I can't remember the exact year, just that it was turn of the century. I recall that it was all-out survival mode. Instinctively, I understood that I had to blend in if I was going to make it to day two."

At this point, our friend begins to sob. And I mean sob. Tears stream down his face. I'm so uncomfortable that I wish that I was sitting anywhere else but where I'm sitting right now. Flynn reaches out for the fallen young man and holds him. I've concluded that sometimes the most effective form of communication is to say nothing at all.

"You really can't remember anything else about that bag?" Flynn whispers.

Booker shakes his head. The mystery surrounding the long-gone treasure continues to fascinate us, but it remains elusive. I can't shake my gut feeling that some old soul in this town had something to do with it.

As our makeshift powwow draws to a close, our thoughts move toward having fun at the pool. I'm game for a much-needed break.

"Who's texting me?" Glancing down at my screen, I notice Andrew's name, along with a message. "Hurry to pool. He's here." While I would love to believe that the "he" in question could really mean many different individuals, I know it means only one thing. Jean Lafitte is poolside. Despite our ongoing conversation, I don't hesitate interrupting. After informing the group about what is going on a few floors below us, we're on our way.

I don't know how to describe my impending feelings about coming face-to-face with a legendary villain. What introductions does one even attempt to make to someone who has singlehandedly destroyed coastlines and amassed enough money to guarantee a safe exile for centuries to come? How will I even know it's him when I see him? I wonder if he will be the guy wearing buckled leather boots and an oversized belt circa GAP 1800s.

Before I can overthink things, we are walking out to the pool area. Rihanna is playing, and the pool is packed. I notice a super-hot waitress winking at me as I pass by. Just as I'm getting my hopes up, Booker crashes me back down to reality, informing me that she's off limits. Evidently, she's two hundred years old and counting. You can't win 'em all. Finally, I see Andrew and Dax sitting in the hot tub with their elbows casually tucked behind them. Things must not be too dire if they're able to focus on relaxation instead of possible mayhem.

As we approach, I notice Shea and Booker glancing over their shoulders as they approach from the dimly lit thoroughfare. Wonder no more. There he sits, accompanied by a cherry-colored drink with a little paper umbrella floating in it. Wow. Maybe I gave this guy way too much street cred. If it hadn't been for a couple of sketchy pics I saw online, I would have thought our pirate was just another middle-aged tourist taking a break after a week spent working inside a cubicle. He isn't wearing any shoes, his shirt is some campy thing that he obviously picked up in some souvenir shop (or stole), and his swim trunks are too long. So last season. I understand I sound shallow to be thinking about all these things at this particular moment, but in a weird way, it helps me gain some much-needed confidence. At least I look good.

Shea and Booker don't miss a beat and immediately fish our group's two youngest from the water. Shea whispers in Andrew's ear. Seconds later, the boys gather their clothes and wrap themselves up with their terry-cloth towels. Both of them march over to where we are. Jeal's gaze never leaves us. He grins before taking an extended sip from his cocktail. Who knows? Maybe we can get this guy so liquored up that he won't have any recollection of why he's here. Wouldn't that be nice? Somehow, I doubt it.

Then, right before my eyes, a disturbing thing happens. The chaise lounge supporting the man's six-foot frame seems to shift shapes. The metal frame grows ever so slightly, and the upper section develops long willowy arms. I can't even begin to fathom what I'm witnessing. The long limbs sprout equally long hands with even longer fingers. I blink, thinking my vision will soon return to normal. Silly me, I guess this is his normal.

Jeal doesn't miss a beat. He stares at our crew while seemingly enjoying the masseuse that was once his chair. The bony fingers press into his bare shoulders, and the crook sighs. Wow! He is taunting us while simultaneously receiving a massage. I detect that he is also trying to intimidate us. I hate to admit it, but he might be succeeding.

Thomas

I have never laid eyes on Jean Lafitte in any other era except for the past. How peculiar to see him now. Gosh, I haven't ever seen his bare legs. Back in the day, one would never have left the house without being dressed in appropriate attire. My, how things have changed. Women wouldn't think about sunbathing on a beach while displaying their ankles. Goodness knows that too much sun exposure was an absolute no-no. In fact, that was a sign of one's lower-class status. Here I'm witnessing Lafitte half-dressed and watching him shake his feet to the sounds of today's music. I begin to question whether the man even notices my presence. I suppose that by now, even Jean understands that I have no knowledge of where his long-lost stash is stowed.

No, the pirate's focus seems to be glued on Booker. Poor Booker. Say what you want, I feel that he is telling the truth. I don't believe he has any knowledge of where or, more importantly, what has happened to the mysterious satchel. I will take it one step further and say that I don't think he had a clue what was inside the bag. The problem is, we must locate its whereabouts after all these years. This definitely qualifies as a cold trail. I am contemplating all these things in my mind when I notice Booker and Shea walking straight toward their arch nemesis. Are they crazy? I search for hotel security, just in case. Do modern-day cops even arrest half-alive criminals?

As I ponder my many questions, their brief conversation ends, and the two head back to where we are gathered. We ask them all sorts of questions before Booker speaks. "Look, the man wants his stuff back. Here's the thing: it's not his loot! He stole it to begin with. He's throwin' around all kinds of threats, you know?"

Andrew grins. "Dude is lit, and he's angry."

"We're just going to have to figure out where the treasure is before he does," Shea says. "I guess it really belongs with the rightful owners, whomever that may be."

"Aren't they dead?" Andrew asks. "I'm sorry, but how is all this our problem? No offense, Booker, you've got a problem, but . . .."

We all decide it best to cut Andrew off from any more of his unfiltered thoughts. There is no plus to come from a bunch of finger pointing. Booker is already agitated. "I don't know what happened to it!" Alrighty then; he couldn't be more crystal clear.

As things settle down, Shea questions Booker once again. "What *can* you remember for sure from that night? Who else has ties to any of this?"

The former slave dissolves into a relapse of the moments so long ago. He paces back and forth, searching for some music on his phone. As we listen to Kanye belt out the "Paris Ballad," our friend begins. "I recall showing up in some awful water, the animals, the rain, and the moon still shining through it all."

"Yeah, the drool," Flynn interjects. "I so remember all that. Hard to forget." We all shoot Flynn a look, and he forces himself to stay quiet as Booker delves even deeper.

"I jump in and check, not really knowing what to expect but still clinging to that bag. I swear, it's like those animals knew something was going down. They almost had a glee in their eyes. Have you ever been face-to-face with a donkey? Don't answer. The rain was coming down hard, and it was getting cold! I totally blacked out." Booker collapses into a semi-fetal position, all the energy seemingly sucked out of his body. "Then, I woke up!" His following expletive startles us. He goes on to explain that while he was never soaking wet during his crossing over; he arrived completely drenched in the hotel kitchen. "I felt like an alien." I didn't have the heart to tell him that he might as well have been from outer space.

It is about now that Booker's memory appears to get fuzzy. He describes his fear of not knowing where he was coupled with his hesitation over all the lurking eyes on him. Self-preservation is what one typically calls it. The former slave describes how he leapt out of the kitchen sink, which was filled with peeled carrots and potatoes, before sprinting out the first door he could find. He was no longer in the early 1800s. After taking a quick look around and trying to acclimate himself to his new surroundings, Booker surmised that he had been pushed to some date in the future. I imagine his initial fears didn't allow him time to ask many questions. Eventually, the hard worker adjusted to his new world quite well. This world was the turn of the century. Booker describes his determination to force himself to be part of a new era. How things had changed. This world would introduce new methods of transportation, computers, and, thank you from above, cell phones! Evidently, the one thing that never factored into Booker's initial thought process was whether he would age. He may believe in a new millennium, but he will always be the ripe old age of twenty-one. At least he's legal.

⁑ Travel

Shea (*Night Five*)

The seriousness of the last hour is grating on all of us. We need some escapism and to put pirates and ghosts aside at least for a few hours. Some opt for the pool, but the rest of us are stoked to hit the beach after dark. There can't be a person around who is immune to the smell of the ocean and the vibe of people wearing barely there clothing. We hide our Birks behind some bushes. I just need to feel the sand. Flynn and I get a head start, and I can already feel my body beginning to unwind. As our pace slows down, we hear someone shout to us. "Hey, you guys want to join us?"

In the distance, we spot a small bonfire with a few girls scattered around it. I don't mind receiving an invite and appreciate it even more if the girls are easy on the eyes. They are. Flynn flashes me a smile. Our lazy pace soon picks up.

"Want something to drink?" a brunette asks. She hands me a sweet tea, and I feel for the sand and sit alongside a great distraction. Life is good. Her name is Riley, and she is visiting from Dallas. I'm instantly taken in by her smile and warm eyes. Riley is hoping to major in dance in the fall. She tells me these details while stretching her legs into a move that I could never do. She is naturally pretty with long dark hair and a great tan. Girls like her don't even need much makeup.

Thirty minutes pass, and we have been talking non-stop. I almost forget that Matt and Andrew are still planning on meeting up with us. Then I hear Andrew's voice. I have completely erased all thoughts of Jean Lafitte from my mind.

"Hey, Shea. Remember us?" Andrew asks. Of course, he knows good and well that he is bordering on annoying. Still, I play it cool and do the introductions. Our group has expanded, and the low flames make the perfect backdrop to tonight's mood, depicting a lazy summer night. Riley is a total babe and even laughs at my jokes. I'm beginning to think she is close to perfection. I'm becoming increasingly worried that I might be approaching the "Thomas" territory, only he has been carrying his emotions with him for two hundred years.

As the fire spews some sparks every once in a while, I can't envision how this evening will ever come to an end. The sounds of the waves beginning their descent into high tide coupled with the looming darkness turns the scene into seriously romantic territory. I could go on and on if it wasn't for the fact that the darkening skies seem a bit too all-consuming because of a heavy fog quickly approaching us. Unfortunately, the haze is impairing my vision of Riley. Why does all this seem to be getting weirder and weirder? Am I the only one who notices it?

Evidently not. Within seconds, I can't even make out the ground beneath me, let alone anyone sitting next to me. Panic overtakes our idyllic little utopia. Everyone jumps to their feet and scrambles around to regain their bearings. Andrew yells for me.

"Andrew, just come toward my voice," I instruct him. If this wasn't such an intense situation, it might rank alongside a great game of

Marco Polo. I hear my little brother and expect it's him who is yanking at my arm. It isn't. It's Riley. While I would like nothing more than to hold her hand, this is not the way I envisioned it to happen. I grasp her hand while repeating my pleas for Andrew to try and find me in the thick smog. Suddenly, I feel a huge force that sends me straight to the ground. Well, at least my brother located me. "Stay with me, and don't leave my side!"

After a few more seconds of sheer craziness, I decide that the best solution is for all of us to gather together in ankle-deep water, away from the bonfire. One by one, the familiar voices of our group grow closer together. Booker instructs everyone to remain connected with each other. It sounds like he has remained on the sand. "Stay right where you are, and let me try figuring this out!"

It is becoming painfully clear that something much more ominous than bad lighting is responsible for what is going on. Before I can verbalize my suspicions, I detect a figure looming directly behind our immortal friend. Booker senses the intruder and doesn't even dignify his presence before addressing him. "What exactly do you want from all us?" I have to believe his rhetorical question will go unanswered. The treasure is the only thing on Lafitte's mind.

Jean stands in place, totally composed. "Booker, you must understand how deeply you have hurt and betrayed me. Words cannot begin to describe my disillusionment with you. I trusted you. I valued you. You betrayed me, stabbed me in the back. Isn't that what they say nowadays?"

Booker appears unfazed. I get the impression he is more than prepared to confront the person who has caused him so many years of suffering. "You owned me, nothing more. You were the definition of a monster." He turns and faces the same arched brows that haunted him a century earlier. "I'm not in debt to you and care nothing about you."

With those simple words, the shock on Jean's face is evident, and he appears to have had the wind knocked out of him. The once-revered figure seems to be trying to regain his composure and regain control of the situation. It finally seems to dawn on the two men that they have an audience. Lafitte takes several baby steps backwards before speaking. "Booker, remind yourself that Evelyne rewarded me with some ingenious spells. Awesome, even. I have always been partial to one in particular. You know, where the mind can play some crazy tricks. Isn't it a shame when people allow their innermost fears to overcome reality?"

Booker continues looking at his deranged former master with disgust. He doesn't speak. I doubt he ever blinks. This non-verbal communication does doing little to alleviate any concerns that are creeping inside my head. I wonder what all this means. The fear factor jumps into overdrive when Booker tells us to clear our minds from all things that frighten us. "Don't allow a single scary idea into your consciousness, and try releasing all your fears. Block everything out, if you can." I wonder if Booker has been to this rodeo once or twice before. Either way, I don't like it.

The fog continues engulfing us, but eventually, we are able to make out each other's outlines. I swear, even Riley's foggy figure is hot. Unfortunately, Lafitte still won't shut up. "To whom vengeance belongeth, judge of the earth, fools will you be wise . . . knoweth the inner thoughts of a person, use their multitude of these things, reward me, and delight my soul."

Our voodoo-loving pirate whips out a black candle from the inside pocket of his swim trunks and then lights it. As I try to untangle the words he just spoke, he tosses the lit candle into the ocean. Slowly, it begins to float away. Lafitte releases the most awful-sounding laugh. "Be careful tonight," he warns. Then he jogs back toward the pathway that leads to the pool. I really can't stand him.

It isn't long before Flynn asks the obvious. "What does any of that mean? Are we supposed to be scared of something? I hate to admit it, but I'm kind of confused here."

Our attention zeroes in on Booker. "Clear your thoughts," he says. "Think about unicorns, Whataburger, anything."

That sounds simple enough. Don't think. Let's face it, some of us are better at that than others. As the mist rises, we make our way back to the bonfire. It occurs to me that I have no idea how long we are supposed to remain void of thoughts.

Wouldn't you know it, my question proves to be short lived. In the distance, several palms begin swaying violently, and it doesn't appear to be from any coastal breeze. Something large appears to be pushing them from behind. I take a deep breath and wonder what we have gotten ourselves into.

⁺⁺ Box Out

Matt

Whether the guy with the eyepatch really believes in any of his spells is irrelevant. Booker encourages us to seek immediate shelter, and I must admit, this has me a bit concerned. I'm standing here just waiting for the unknown to occur before I hear several loud grunts. The turmoil is coming from a wooded area a few hundred yards away. I grasp the person's hand next to me, completely unaware of whose hand I'm holding. I'm beginning to understand why it's so difficult for some kids to give up their security blankets. The trees in the distance are still moving, and the cause does not appear to be any natural occurrence.

Booker turns and faces us. "Who didn't erase their thoughts? Seriously, just fess up. I want a heads-up, so I can prepare for what's coming for us!"

We shift our eyes back and forth between one another, imagining that an explanation will magically appear. How I wish it was that easy. The next thing I detect is a blurry vision of some large hands. Let me reiterate, large! The fingers attached to these hands are ever so carefully peeling the tops of the green palms backwards, enabling the rest of its giant body to move past them. Great. This creature must be super-sized. Despite the late hour and the lack of light, the moon shines just brightly enough to give us our first glimpse of the impending danger.

I don't know. I tried, I really did. Unfortunately, everyone seems to know that the one person unable to shut out their scariest dream is me. Seriously, how can anyone expect someone to just erase all bad thoughts when put on the clock like this? I must say, kudos to whomever thought up this little spell, because not in a million years would I have believed it could actually work. It did. How I wish this little scheme could have clicked with someone else. I hate being the person who blew it!

After everyone catches a glimpse of the giant being moving toward us, it doesn't take long before all eyes are on me. Yes, I am the culprit. Perhaps it was the uni-brow, the ten-foot-long beard, or maybe the oversized muscular arms that gave it away. Nevertheless, the creature is pushing toward us. He appears to be a huge Iron Man compilation of every single fear I have ever entertained in a basketball game. The twelve-foot bionic image is every shooting guard's worst nightmare and then some. I'm not detecting that my creation speaks any recognizable language. In fact, I believe that if a cross between Freddy Krueger and an A-list athlete exists, this is it.

"Seriously, Matt. This is your biggest fear? Did you dream this up one night after shooting bricks, or something?" Shea shouts.

Meanwhile, the hairy, sweaty Amazon continues toward us. While the scenario might seem humorous, it is not. Its nostrils flare, and an unpleasant liquid drips from its mouth. What I'm witnessing is positively frightening and bordering on grotesque!

Booker instructs us to remain perfectly still and to keep our eyes closed. "This is not real. It is only real if you allow it to be. Otherwise, the image will soon vanish."

Easy for him to say! I can smell its sweat permeating its purple jersey. At this point, I have no idea what team this dude thinks he's representing. He is simply gross!

Our makeshift monster lumbers forward, never once looking behind him. It would be no use trying to outrun him. His strides are almost a half court per leg, and those arms are able to scoop us up and toss us beyond the nearest dunes. Why couldn't I have taken up cooking during the fifth grade? Unfortunately, as his "creator," I assume I am his intended target. It is now or never. All my life, I have heard that the mental game is just as important as the physical aspect. It appears I'm about to find out.

The beast hovers over me, and I feel my windswept hairstyle beginning to move thanks to its labored breathing. I sense the substitute player bending down as he tries getting face to face with me. Whew! His smell is proof enough that I need to abide by my mom's wishes and take showers after every workout. I'm barely able to keep my dinner down. My eyes remain tightly closed, and my focus remains on this caricature of NBA greatness come to life. How can this possibly be my demise? I refuse to succumb to some hodgepodge of wannabe players! No, I decide it's time to confront this monster once and for all!

"If you really are all that, you would be one of the greats, not just a bunch of facial hair! You don't intimidate me!" The creature stands perfectly still, speechless. Maybe because he can't speak. I don't know. Either way, after a few long moments, the fog that had engulfed us begins to float around the not-so-gentle giant. Piece by piece, the image of this future NBA Hall of Famer begins flaking away into the hazy winds.

It takes a few moments before I'm able to take a deep breath. It really is mind over matter. What is the famous slogan displayed on the Warriors' shirts? "Strength in Numbers." This phrase proves to be spot on as it pertains to our current situation. If the motto works for them, I pray it will work magic for us. I sincerely hope my clan appreciates how I just saved their lives!

Shea

The monster disappears right before our eyes. Unfortunately, no one is sure where Jeal has run off to. It goes without saying that none of the current turmoil will stop until this age-old mystery is solved. Since neither Booker nor Thomas seems to have any recollection of many of the events that occurred so many evenings ago, our focus must shift to someone not experiencing amnesia. As much as I'd love to pull out a lengthy contact list of individuals fitting that category, no such luck. The other obstacle facing us is that none of the hotel's current employees was even born yet (as far as I know). The night in question marked our friend Booker's first clocking in.

We make our way back up to the pool. Suffice it to say that my formerly carefree ambience has been shattered by recent events. Riley is keeping up with me stride for stride. "The only surefire thing in life is love and friendship," she whispers. My heart skips a few beats, and I like this girl even more. Her words of wisdom also spark a thought. One soul might remember a few important facts regarding that fateful night.

Simone. How I wish I could quiz anyone in the world besides her, but it is what it is. When Booker arrived, Simone had already staked her claim as the never-ending houseguest at the luxurious Galvez. Even if she didn't witness everything herself, she may have a sense of what went down. There must be a few perks for being constantly dead and able to float around the hallways as she does.

I hang back from the group a bit, hoping to corner Thomas for a private one-on-one. Thomas is still amused by the latest Hulu film showing on Andrew's phone. It takes my grabbing his elbow and stopping him in his tracks before he even notices my presence. "Oh, sorry. I was stunned by what all you call streaming. It truly is like a stage play but inside this tiny box. Incredible."

I force myself to remain patient with him. "T, there might be someone with whom we can speak with who remembers something important from that night."

Thomas seems honored to have acquired a new nickname. "Oh, do tell. This is becoming like a fun little game of Clue." I have to wonder how this guy would react to a nail-biting match on the court. The difference in our language is becoming rather entertaining.

Thomas and I are standing at the base of the pool's entrance, where no one else is able to overhear our conversation. While our newly minted Mr. T. may be a bit giddy, wanting to go sleuthing, his bubble bursts after I say, "Simone." The anticipated silence overcomes us both. Simone must know something and might even be able to recall the cast of characters involved that night. "I don't think I'm saying anything too crazy when I tell you that she might not be totally honest with anyone but you."

Thomas looks a bit hesitant, and it becomes quite obvious that his little confidence boost a few minutes beforehand has all but evaporated. "We were just beginning to get back on track, Shea. Every topic I have Googled suggests that we look to the future and not remain stuck in the past." Wouldn't you know it, Thomas has been living in our world for less than a day, and he has already mastered the internet. After a few more minutes of convincing, the guy seems to see the light. None of us can move forward if we don't shut the doors to this particular past.

"Well, we do have a private dinner date scheduled for midnight. I must admit that it will be a cheap date due to the fact that she no longer eats. Anyway, I will tactfully ask her after I throw a couple back. I hope this plan is acceptable to you."

I simply nod. After all, I really don't have too many options anymore.

⁞ Layup

Matt

"Who has a dinner date at midnight? That's when a brother should be hitting the clubs. No wonder Thomas never could figure out the girls," Booker exclaims. Booker is still going off on his tirade regarding his comrade's dating techniques, while the rest of us are much more concerned about finding some answers before our games begin tomorrow. Let us not forget to factor in Thomas's insecurities about what he should wear. Suddenly, he goes from vintage clothing to the latest frat boy ensemble. I must remember to tell Shea to make sure his borrowed threads are on loan only. Besides all that, I don't think I have ever seen his girl wear anything but sheer white dresses. It's not like she's dressing to impress.

I'm surprised that I'm not wired after having to save everyone's life earlier, but I'm only interested in trying to research the teams we have yet to play. I strive to be totally absorbed back into my former safe world again. Right on cue, my wishful thinking is broken as Thomas emerges fresh from his shower and clean shaven. Good for us that he has just watched Golden State secure their second straight championship. His hair went from 1800 clean-cut to a newly buzzed flattop, complete with a tiny goatee. The room smells like a bad trip through a department store's cologne section, and the dude has the nerve to wear my favorite shirt. Seriously, that's enough! I sense that Shea is reading my thoughts, as he quickly reminds us what the big purpose is here. Easy for Shea to say; the shirt in question isn't his. If Thomas ruins it, he pays for it. I'm just saying.

I slap the hard copies of tomorrow's brackets down in front of me, knowing full well that a lecture is soon to follow. I wonder if anyone else has noticed that we may be playing the local witch doctor's son in the finals, if all goes down as expected. Won't that be loads of fun? Shea corrals us all together to remind us of the importance of this so-called date night. Thomas might be coasting through, but the rest of us want to figure some things out. "Thomas, obviously, a lot has gone down between you and Simone. None of us—trust me, man, none of us denies that your love is real. Think about it: this is why we all risked everything. We want you to hook back up with her," Shea says. I believe that the one omission in Shea's speech is the fact that no one else is brave enough to attempt a long-term thing with this girl.

Thomas seems to understand what he must do. To his credit, the guy really does love Simone. I'm still a bit fuzzy on the difference between the ghost thing and the time travelers, but I have discovered that it is best not to ask too many questions. If others think this plan is doable, then who am I to doubt? I give the guy one last reassuring hug and dust off his back, literally. There is no need to show up wrinkled. I believe his hair gel might be a bit stiff, but overall, he looks ready. Simone would be a fool to play too hard to get, and we all know how some of these chicas play one too many games.

The date is set to take place on the rooftop. It may sound incredibly romantic, but it is the same rooftop that saw Simone take her feelings one step too far many years ago. Booker has arranged for a small table to be set up, complete with an expensive bottle of wine. (Can she even drink?) No matter, Thomas requested a bit of bar food and chose a few decadent desserts to put an exclamation point on the evening. Secretly, I take a few notes.

Andrew

We are all aware of the sweet little get-together taking place a few floors above us. Thomas seemed so nervous before he left, but he was excited. I'm sure that *so* many years of waiting before finally having the opportunity to meet up with your long-lost love must be overwhelming. I wonder if this is how I would feel if I reconnected with the girl from the pool last year from Port A. Anyway, we're all on standby, pretending to be busy.

BOOM!

Booker needs no other warning before he jumps up and sprints out the door. The noise in question sounded like something being thrown around above us. While I would love to believe it's nothing more than a few college guys throwing some chairs into the pool below, my gut tells me it's much more sinister.

We all make our way up using the exterior stairs. Booker is adamant about not alerting anyone with any unnecessary elevator lights. We make it to the top and push the metal door ajar. Experience warns me to try to predict what I might be walking into. Let's face it, around here, surprises are seldom good ones.

We peek around the corner as we try to grasp the situation. Unfortunately, my first image is the rear end of an aging pirate wearing long socks with his Birkenstocks. Yuck! As I look past him, I see the loved-up couple. Thomas appears to be standing between Simone and our party crasher. If I was old enough to be a betting guy, I'd say that words have already been said. There aren't many lights up here, so I haven't figured out if anyone has detected our busting in on the scene. I hope not.

One thing is for sure: Linda Blair has nothing on this chick. I can only assume that these two have not laid eyes on each other since that night in question. I don't know what Jeal was thinking would happen once Simone finally caught sight of him. Surely, he must have had anticipated that Simone would be a bit angry, to put it mildly. We notice that the formidable man's confidence and stature seems to shrink after the ghost bride locks eyes onto him. Ever so slowly, the tall pirate quietly shuffles backwards, and it appears that he might be rethinking his plan, hoping to locate an exit. Simone seems to have other ideas in mind.

As much as I would like to return to the anonymity of the fifth floor, it feels like some force is preventing me from moving a single sore muscle. My next plan is to close my eyes, as if I'm being forced to watch the latest scary movie. But as with the movie, I can't quit watching.

Simone's figure slowly changes into an eerie display of total hollowness. Sure, she has always been a bit see-through, but I can't recall being able to make out every single bone of her once-mortal frame. Maybe she's rethinking the whole club date. The flowing cloth from her dress, which she was wearing so proudly for Thomas, becomes much more form fitting. Every inch of it is glued to her bones. The most disturbing aspect of all this is her eyes. Her pupils turn into extra-large pitch-black holes cut out in the back of her head. I can actually see the pitch darkness of the night through her skull. I believe that Simone might secure a callback if she was auditioning for a heavy metal band.

At first, the young lady simply floats along with her head facing toward the cement floor. Despite her creepiness, she still appears somewhat apprehensive. Every once in a while, she peeks up with those eye sockets of hers, taking a quick inventory of her surroundings. It occurs to me that, through all this, Thomas has still not uttered a single word. I have a gut feeling that Thomas's silence might be an indication of some things that are about to come. I assume these things will not be good.

Jeal appears to be feeling the same as the rest of us are. The pirate is searching for something inside his khaki shorts. He tries to remain jovial while still pleading with the girl. "Now, Simone, honey, let's talk. First of all, my dear, despite everything, may I say how beautiful you still are." He whispers to her while pretending that none of us can overhear their semi-private conversation. "You haven't aged a day."

Unfortunately for Simone's killer, the words fall on deaf ears. (In this sister's mind, the pirate might as well have thrown her off the building after what he told her during that infamous visit.)

As she stops inches in front of Lafitte, time seems to stand still. I wonder if the grifter's hollow words might have gotten through to her. She raises her face to meet his, and they look at one another for a few seconds. Jeal smiles slightly as he reaches for her hand. Well, this is truly shocking. I never saw this coming. I don't think she did either. Short-lived. The sound that follows is the most deafening noise I have ever heard. In fact, it is so high in pitch that the entire building begins to sway, and the clouds above light up like fireballs.

Then, out of nowhere, a swarm of flies appears. At first, they appear to be a bad case from the Weather Channel. I'm tempted to reach for my imaginary umbrella. It is only after the buzzing noises become so severe that I realize these are not, in fact, low-riding water droplets but a huge mass of insects flying right at us. It is impossible for me to see anything. I have always heard that every culture views these pesky insects as a precursor to death. Funny, but I don't think any of this is a coincidence.

When I look up, Simone's face has all but vanished. Sure, the outline of her head is still visible, but the rest of her features are absent, except for those awful black holes. Then everything changes. The wayward girl is sporting a mouth. A smile emerges, but it isn't one that is welcoming any guests to come watch a game at the house. No. All she's lacking is some deep crimson lipstick to complete the "Joker" look. The sounds from the flies is getting louder, and they're headed directly for the pirate. If I was Lafitte, I would take cover, and now.

Without warning, her dark eyes and wicked grin seem to implode into her head. While my eyes are still fixated onto the atrocities of Simone's facial features, hundreds of flies pour out of her mouth. I will never complain about the filth from farm animals again. I feel dirt spraying against my skin along with sharper shots coming from objects being pummeled against me. Somehow, I manage to sneak a peek and notice the startled look on Jean Lafitte's face. At this moment, we're perched on top of this old building trying to grasp anything we can, hoping like crazy not to be blown off.

Then a scream turns the blood in our veins to ice. I knew she had it in her! Thomas lunges beneath the table, which just recently displayed a dozen red roses. As the five of us of hold on for dear life, Lafitte is blown backwards. Wow! This girl sure does have some lungs.

The pirate seems a bit embarrassed after being forced back onto his rear. (I admit I can see how a guy's ego might be bruised after that.) Then he pulls out the mysterious object, for which he has been so diligently searching, from deep inside his pockets. It is a cross with a circle around the middle. He shoves it directly into Simone's face, and all the heavy winds and terrifying tremors cease. As I watch in disbelief, a subtle white mist envelopes our girl, and she begins to lose her bony image. Simone floats from side to side, appearing to be a bit tipsy. Do they serve Cosmopolitans on the rooftop? I don't think any of us are prepared for a Simone who has had one drink too many. It's too bad we've been so fixated on the resident ghost, because as we look over to the spot we last saw our popular villain, he's long gone.

Thomas

After finally regaining our composure, the next decision to be made is to get off this roof. I have concluded that nothing positive comes from being up here. Simone told me that she feels the need for a few moments to herself after what just transpired. I understand completely. It's a safe bet that my newfound friends have found the recent events unsettling, to say the least. Honestly, I could have called this, so to speak. How does one say, it has been a long time coming? I'm sure Lafitte is searching for the same answers as the rest of us. What happened to the fortune? All this is seemingly turning into a finale of the *Amazing Race*. Where is the so-called moneymaker?

After it becomes apparent that Jean has bailed, we decide to make our way downstairs to the kitchen. Booker is convinced that this will be our best bet for ensuring privacy. Evidently, not too many people are using room service, because most are still visiting seaside bars. I wish someone would have warned me what I was about to walk into on this side of the fence. Where did the donkey come from? Does anyone actually believe this equine animal is going to go unnoticed hanging out in the dry goods area? I believe I'm a bit more important than their new pet.

Andrew remains with Mr. Ed, feeding him tomorrow's stash of vegetables. The rest of us congregate around the fridge area. The coolness feels wonderful after developing a thick veil of sweat from all the recent activity. I'm not stupid. I know what is expected of me. I must continue questioning Simone. After all, we were so rudely interrupted.

I feel overwhelmed. Here I am, a man living in a time that is not my own. Looking around me, I wonder how many people out here are from different centuries, different worlds. Unlike Simone, no one can detect any difference between Booker and the other employees. He has a body that is devoid of any abnormalities. In fact, he is a gorgeous specimen. Glancing down the main corridor, I catch a glimpse of the infamous Bernardo, permanently trapped inside his portrait. Why is he still inside a gilded frame, and yet his daughter can cruise around at will? Maybe I will never fully understand all these unanswered mysteries. After all, I can't even explain my own current zip code. As I continue delving into my innermost thoughts, Bernardo smiles.

⁝ Turnover

Andrew *(Game Time)*

I can't begin to count how many gyms and tournaments I have been to. Basketball really is a way of life. Once again, I find myself sitting in the stands preparing to support my brothers. Next year, I'm going to be suited up as well. After a few seconds, my mental game is broken because of a spectator making his way into the stands. Seriously? Does anyone expect me to believe that a crazy pirate knows anything about hoops? Now the man has the nerve to show up live? This guy is only attempting to stir up even more trouble.

At this point, Booker spots him too. He scopes out the gym, making certain our man showed up alone. I'm still unsure who all is on this so-called roster.

It is almost two minutes until half time, and the game grows increasingly close. Too close for my taste. It's the inevitable moment when parents lose their calm exteriors and voice their frustration. The pristinely dressed suburban mother with the expensive handbag turns into her alter-ego evil stepsister. You would never believe her carefully chosen rhetoric could be meant for whomever her son is guarding. It isn't pretty.

The game is tied and headed for overtime. Matt pulls off a shot, and the ball is straight net. "Bang, bang!" Shea says to no one in particular. Quickly, the other team heads down to their end and repeats the process. Tied again. Flynn grabs the pass and charges down to make one last attempt. The ball is up, and it looks good.

All I detect are arms waving high in the air before the perfectly arched shot is slammed down. "Goaltending!" our coach yells. The referee doesn't appear too happy about any of what is now going down. I sense things are going to get a bit interesting. He shakes his head as the final buzzer blares, indicating the clock to be set to two minutes. Oh no. Coach jumps to his feet and beelines to the center table, followed by his assistant. I don't think I've ever seen our main man so agitated. The two men stand face to face, separated by mere inches. "Haven't you ever heard of goaltending? Look in the books!"

"There has to be something that enables me to throw his butt entirely out of this game! Is there? Did he just ask me for one too many time-outs? I think I just heard his sorry self ask me that." The ref won't stop asking the officials these questions and many more. Meanwhile, our second man in charge, Kevin, dutifully steps into the heated exchange before Coach picks him up and sets to one side as if he is nothing more than a rag doll. The noise inside the gym keeps getting louder, and pretty much everyone's attention is directed toward the sideshow that was once a basketball game. I almost forget we were blessed with our curious outcast before all the latest shenanigans distracted us.

I look around wondering what Lafitte's reaction might be to all this. Finally, out of the corner of my eye, I notice a middle-aged man scooting down the bleachers, politely mouthing "excuse me" to all those around him. He is sporting a huge grin while making his exit.

As his feet hit the floor, I notice him dusting something off from one of his palms and then wiping his hand on the front of his shirt. He appears to be rather pleased with himself. Could it be that everything transpiring right now is due to the magical handiwork of a vindictive pirate?

I'm dying to find out where the guy is headed but also don't want to miss out on a great finale. Too many options! I make up my mind when I notice Booker hit the ground in sly pursuit of Lafitte. I try keeping pace with him, but he is already out the door. Maybe I should stay put, but seriously, how fun would that be?

Soon, I'm outside and feel the scorching summer heat hit my skin. From a distance, I see Booker is clutching his phone in one hand while making his way to the beach. He looks both ways before crossing the busy highway and flopping down on a waiting rock. His cell is glued to his ear. It appears that Booker's current conversation is rather tense. He shakes his head as if he's trying to emphasize an important point and paces around in the sand. I can't decide if I should join him or remain in my carefully crafted cover spot.

A few more minutes pass before I conclude that all this detective work is way too slow for me. Besides all that, my foot is falling asleep. As I stand up and rub my arch, I see a second figure approaching the beach. At first, I assume he is one more kid excited to hit the waves, until I recognize his distinctive profile. It's Caesar, the midget from the pier who gave me my stash on that first night. Well, now things might be getting a bit more interesting. Booker makes it seem like the two of them barely see each other. It strikes me as odd that these two are deciding to hang out together today of all days. I thought Booker's plate was kind of full. I reach for my phone, hoping to establish some concrete evidence regarding this impromptu meeting. I believe this particular occasion justifies use of the zoom button.

Luckily for me, the subjects in question don't even realize I'm recording anything—or that I'm even near them, for that matter.

Feeling bold, I inch even closer. My busywork has morphed into true "Mortal Combat." Instead of a weapon, I have an iPhone—the latest model, of course. With my adrenaline kicking into high gear, I fail to sense impending danger. Too bad. I hate being caught off guard.

I feel a huge tug on my arm, forcing me to drop everything. Spinning around using every spin-cycle trick I have, I see that the source of my discomfort is none other than the twisted villain himself. No matter which way I turn, his grip on me gets tighter. Lafitte laughs his menacing laugh. "You don't think you can escape me, do you, little man?"

I hate to admit it, but he is probably correct. I feel stuck as I try one last-ditch effort to finagle myself away from his grip. Fine. I throw my head back and release the highest-pitched scream that has ever left my mouth. Even I am surprised by the noise. (I'm sure many dogs will seek emotional therapy after what they've been forced to hear.) I can't imagine there is an individual within a half mile of here who hasn't turned their attention to the parking lot in which I am standing.

The only good news is that the intended recipient of my glass-shattering yell spots us. My gut feeling is that we may have formed a real brotherhood. I wave my arms while Lafitte tries to haul me off somewhere. I'm determined not to make this easy for him.

Booker and Caesar break into a full-blown sprint, oblivious to any oncoming cars. I suppose I would have zero fear too if I was immune to any injuries, like they are. Sweat pours off Booker as he leaps over vehicles. I just wish there was a rim somewhere nearby. That would be quite a show.

Jeal has me in a painfully tight embrace before stopping and facing his pursuers. We are all backed in an alley as Booker looks his former boss in the eyes, showing no signs of fear. "Put him down. Now!"

Lafitte shoves me behind his back with his large clammy hands. He stands in front of Booker with defiance written across his face. "Stop right there, if you know what's good for this little guy. You of all people should know I'm not kidding around here." Jeal's arm extends in front of him as he continues, "Let's play a little game, shall we? You do remember how much I enjoy some good old-fashioned parlor fun?"

At this point, Caesar finally catches up to the rest of us, panting heavily. Suffice it to say, there won't be many scouts looking to sign him the next go around. My kidnapper chuckles while turning his attention to the small man. "You made it, I see." Booker is not amused, and frankly, I'm growing tired of feeling bullied. Booker interrupts the man's carefully crafted speech and asks him what he wants. The only positive news to my ears at this moment would be reassurance for my safety.

The tall pirate continues to shield me from my potential rescuers while, once again, digging into his pocket. What is it with this guy and his little bag of tricks? How deep are his pockets, anyway? "Oh, look here, Booker. I just uncovered one of the few earthly possessions you ever had, this glass bead bracelet. Didn't you once tell me that this was your mother's?"

The pain etched into Booker's face is almost unbearable. The thief tosses the trinket high in the sky. I'm not certain it will ever come down.

"Air ball. Nice shot." My comments are highly inappropriate, but he had it coming. Lafitte's grip intensifies.

"This is fairly simple, you two. I even believe my request is something that you can wrap your heads around. You can take little man back, but I want what's mine. I want what you stole from me in the first place. If you can do that for me, I'll even return him with a juicy hot dog in his hand." His last statement seems to amuse him, and he chuckles.

Booker isn't laughing. "How do you expect to get past me? You can't possibly overtake me, old man."

Here Lafitte goes again. I swear, the dude seriously needs some plain-front shorts void of pockets. Jeal keeps searching for something specific but then swipes through his unkempt hair. He pulls out what can only be described as a bunch of dried leaves. The man needs a comb. While my mind is still fixated on the fact a small herb garden is growing on top of his head, he rubs the scratchy plants together. The next thing I know, I'm no longer standing in an alleyway but am instead sitting inside a windowless room at the Galvez.

From my spot on the couch, I hear water splashing around in the nearby restroom sink. Soon enough, out walks Lafitte. He tells me it will be fruitless to attempt to escape from this place. Fruitless? I will never get into the words he uses. The only thing I can relate to is him offering access to his mini bar. "One last thing, my friend. You had better hope your little team of brothers gets me what I have asked for." Lafitte reaches for a set of keys and leaves the room, locking it from the outside. I must orchestrate a well-crafted plan. However, first I take the loser up on the free grub. Grabbing an ice-cold Snickers, I flop back down on the sofa. I have a feeling this might be a long afternoon.

Shea

I don't think I have ever received any news more unsettling than the words Booker just spoke. Rest assured, no one is going to harm my little brother! We simply have to uncover this secret treasure and return it to Lafitte. I no longer care that this guy needs to be punished for what he has done, past and present. The clock is ticking, and we have only a few hours to figure this out. The one constant in all this seems to be Simone. She is still the one set of eyes who might have witnessed who ended up with the satchel.

As I proceed out the main doors of the hotel lobby, I'm struck by how out of place I feel among the many vacationers. Unlike me, their day surely hasn't been filled with unbearable thoughts of having to rescue a relative from the grips of a known murderer. Instead, the crowds surrounding me are simply excited to be escaping their normal routine. Where did I go wrong?

As I walk, I become convinced that the island's humidity is causing the air to feel at least ten degrees hotter than the thermometer shows. Even the breeze from across the street is not enough to cool things off. I reach for the back of my shirt and dab the moisture from my brow. The stress level is high enough; at least I can still attempt to look good.

Finally, I reach my destination. It is a scary thought, but I have learned way too many things about what makes the mysterious man tick. While others only know Lafitte as a mysterious legend of a man, I have the dubious honor of understanding the deepest desires that are hidden inside his scary mind. I know firsthand the importance of money and material things when it comes to the pirate's liveli-hood. He places no value on relationships, and he is totally driven by winning. I think it's fair to say the man has committed enough sins to land himself inside a prison cell for countless generations. (If the prisons are all booked, maybe there's some space available inside a state hospital.) The thing is, the man isn't entirely unbreakable. He does have a few vices. Jean Lafitte likes a pretty girl, and I know just whom to call.

I enter the back of our adjacent hotel. No one seems to notice me or even care. Before long, I arrive on my chosen floor. Glancing down at my phone, I double check to make sure I'm at the correct location, room 400. I tap on the door a few times before an inviting face opens it and welcomes me inside. It's Riley. As impossible as it may seem, she is even prettier than I remember her being last night. We remain inside the foyer of her room as we quietly finalize our plans. Her hair is half up, half down, and she has some slight tan marks from where her swimsuit straps must have been lying across her shoulders. Darn it. I must remain focused.

"Shea." Riley smiles at me and motions to her friends that she was about to leave for a while. The perspiration running down the back of my neck must give her pause, because she seems to know I need some last-minute reassurance. "It's going to be alright. I know it." How I hate putting Riley in this position. This isn't the ideal way to impress a girl.

┊ Block

Thomas ///

The waiting is always the hardest part. I should know this better than anyone. I have been stuck in limbo, reliving awful events over and over as if they were on a broken movie reel. To keep myself busy, I have decided to fill out an application for the Galvez. I must be qualified to do something around here. Unfortunately, I can't explain all my past employment in too much detail. Let's be honest: my work history includes theft, piracy, even conspiracy. Evidently, these things don't bode well on applications for future employers. Instead, I choose to speak about my management skills and marketing background. I have references from Booker, Caesar, and Eva. Booker reassures me that he is getting me "set up" with a friend of his who will give me some ID. He tells me to just go with it. I hope the picture is good.

As I jot down some of my most memorable experiences, my mind drifts off to a long-ago afternoon, before any tragic events took place. It was hot, no surprise there. In the distance, several storm clouds were blowing in. So many vivid colors lit up the sky. Half the clouds were milky white, while those trailing them were every color of the rainbow. After the kaleidoscope of color, all the remaining clouds were pitch black. The juxtaposition was like nothing I had ever seen. Well, I'm getting a bit ahead of myself.

I walked toward the wooden pier where Lafitte was standing. For some reason, his stature appeared even taller than normal. Maybe he was wearing his favorite block heels. The man always did love a good heel height. Eventually, I was standing directly behind him, not uttering a word. He didn't look back but, obviously, sensed my presence. It was beginning to feel like one of those rare occasions in which I seemed to be more of a friend than an employee. Our predestined evening soon to come would definitely change all that. At that moment, an undeniable magic was floating in the air.

"Thomas, believe it or not, I'm actually going to miss this place. I really thought I would be here for the long haul."

I wasn't quite sure how to respond to his foreboding statement, so I chose to simply nod. It was about that time that I sensed something moving underneath the pier. Trying to maintain my composure, I shuffled toward the center of the rickety boards. Surely, there couldn't be a shark circling in those shallow waters. As I continued my mini breakdance, Jeal let out a boisterous laugh. He laughed so hard that he clutched his midsection while simultaneously slapping my shoulder. "Thomas, you make me laugh. These are some livestock for my dinner parties, should I ever be in short supply." I must have looked thoroughly confused, because Jean followed it up with, "Evelyne thought of it. It's a fabulous idea!"

I proceeded to a spot where the sun's reflection didn't blind me, and I finally saw the peculiar creatures . It was one of the strangest sights I have ever seen. I was looking at numerous chickens, complete with long tails, scurrying around on the ocean floor. Many of them looked as if they were painted the deepest hues of red, yellow, and orange. The sheer craziness of it all left me speechless. An entire barn-yard beneath the water. I was snapped out of it only by Lafitte telling me, "I do hope we can stay in touch after all this is over. I know I can count on you."

I heard his words, but they didn't register.

Shea

Riley and I make our way back to the main entrance of the Galvez. As we scoot past a couple of guys unloading their luggage, I text Booker about our impending arrival. I detect from his response that some serious guilt has been creeping into his conscience.

We enter the infamous room 501, and I'm hit by just how quiet everything is. Andrew isn't there. I take a huge breath before laying out my plan of action. Riley will unveil her unmistakable charm on our favorite pirate while Booker and I follow him back to his hidden crib. Although the game plan seems relatively straightforward, we still must execute our roles perfectly. It's becoming obvious that Riley has been cast in a few school plays. Either that or she has watched one too many episodes of *Gossip Girl* and has mastered some method facial expressions. It takes no time before her hair tossing from side to side is perfectly choreographed, and her Marc Jacobs "Daisy" is sending small whiffs into the air. I don't know why I was so worried that any of this was going to be a bit much for her. The girl is a pro.

As we exit our safe confines, Riley takes one last long look into the mirror, which is hanging by the door. It's like she has all but forgotten we're still watching her, mere extras in this play. She makes one last adjustment to her shorts while giving her backside a quick glance. Booker and I look at each other. "What?" she says a bit defensively. "You want this to work, don't you?"

The group text lights up our phones. It simply states, "POOL." Flynn has been camped out downstairs, trying to blend in with the potted plants. He gives us details about how the old guy is hitting on every waitress he sees. If this summer basketball thing doesn't work out, Flynn might have a future in espionage. Booker and I trail behind Riley, close but not too close.

"Let's go, boys," Riley says. The three of us head over to the stairs. Just as I open the door, I find myself on the receiving end of a massive hug. Matt. Then he turns around and leaves us standing there.

As I walk, my mind can't erase the memory of Matt's embrace. I will be the first to admit that the three of us brothers have experienced a lot together, good and bad. I recall real feelings of envy, anger, irritation and how competitive we can all be toward each other. We have fought over everything at one time or another. The crazy reality is that nothing can break our unique bond. Matt's latest display of emotions is a last-minute reminder as to what is truly at stake right now. I don't need to be told twice. Family is such a peculiar thing.

Riley

This is definitely not the laid-back, relaxing vacay I anticipated when I left Dallas a few days ago. No matter; this is where I want to be. Last night on the beach was memorable, to say the least. Now I have been recruited to participate in the plot of a lifetime! Initially, I was just excited to have Shea seek me out, maybe wanting to pursue something more. Then I discovered that my crush trusts me enough to ask for assistance in helping rescue his little brother. I will make sure that I give this venture 100 percent! I'm wearing my coolest beach outfit, which shouts that I look great but didn't try too hard. I have doused myself with the perfect fragrance and am having a great hair day. The

Hunger Games wouldn't have worked if Katniss had been forced to wear some awful, baggy outfit and not had time to wash her hair.

Like most girls my age, I have already been forced to deal with many self-absorbed guys, and I feel like I'm up to this particular task. I choose to view this assignment as a Gatsby-like experiment. Where do the pirate's needs really lie? Is he truly interested only in money and fortunes? Surely, he is filled with an inner conflict or two, or a dozen. It appears that he places zero value on people, even treating his pack of dogs better than those surrounding him. There is nothing quite like a face from your past to help remind you of who you once were or still are.

I walk casually into the pool are while making sure my phone is fully charged. I have total trust in my wingmen. None of us are naive enough to believe that, should Lafitte unravel our plot, he wouldn't figure out that all of us would be here. That said, I swing my straw tote over my shoulder. First up, locating the perfect lounge chair. My earbuds are tucked inside my ears, but no sound is coming from them. This is my go-to safety distraction. I have mastered this move in many grocery stores. I grab one of the complimentary white towels and find my chair of choice.

As I lay out my belongings, I discreetly scout the scene from behind my polarized glasses. I notice nothing to my right except a few tired mothers who are treating themselves to some much-deserved wine. The center of the pool is overrun by the tween set, a few of them belting out David Perth. I discreetly lift my hand in hopes of locating a nearby waiter while mouthing the words, "Sweet tea, please." I'm overcome with nervous energy and decide it best to keep myself semi-occupied. I reach down for my current beach read, suitably titled, *Beach House Murder.*

After speed reading through the first chapter, I feel a sense of being watched. Sure enough, I spot a middle-aged man located directly across from me. He is sporting a tropical print shirt with clashing swim trunks. I don't detect a black eyepatch though.

"I can do this," I mutter to myself. I watch the man for a few more minutes. I'm ready.

Slowly, and with total ease, I get up from my lounger and walk over to the steps at the shallow end of the pool. Lafitte has tucked himself beneath a large umbrella, which shields his eyes from the sun. I decide to take this up a few notches. I sit down on the first step while tilting my head back, soaking up some rays. Nonchalantly, I scoop up some water and run it over the length of my hair and my legs and take a long, lingering sip of my drink. (I refuse to stoop as low as to ask him to help me apply sunscreen.) Nonetheless, I now have his undivided attention. I pretend to look around, as if I haven't a care in the world. Lafitte smiles at me and positions himself so that I'm forced to notice a new gold watch adorning his wrist. Finally, he makes his move.

As creepy as all this is becoming, I remind myself that, back in his day, the age thing wasn't really a deterrent. I force myself to take a deep breath, ladylike of course, and prepare for the inevitable. The man sits beside me and places his feet directly next to mine under the water. He has his drink with him, and I get a huge whiff of coconut rum.

"Hi, I'm Johnny. I couldn't help but notice you. Nice tan, nice everything."

I want to roll my eyes but somehow abstain. I must remain focused on my mission. I smile as I give him the once over. "Nice to meet you, Johnny. I'm Miranda." (I'm not stupid enough to give him my real name.) He smiles again and lifts his almost-empty glass, signaling for us to toast. Our glasses make the customary clinking noise, and I can't help but wonder if he notices that my choice of cocktail is a Shirley Temple.

I detect Booker and Shea watching our every move from the far end of the pool. I feel secure enough to encourage the pirate to order one more. "To new acquaintances," I say. He obliges, what a shocker.

I'm aware that we are dealing with one of the most intriguing characters, but at this moment, he just seems a bit wasted and not that scary. In fact, I think I was more affected after watching *Get Out*. However, it doesn't escape me that I must not get too comfortable. The only element missing is creepy background music.

I decide it's now or never and I force myself to plant a quick kiss on the man's unshaven cheek. I am overwhelmed by the aroma of his cheap aftershave. I believe our pirate has been doing some shopping since he arrived in our dimension.

"Miranda, if you don't mind, I would like to have some real conversation with you. Can you wait here? I just have to attend to something but will be right back."

The fish seems to have taken the bait. "Of course, Johnny."

Jeal gets up and heads back to the lobby, oblivious to the fact that Booker and Shea are following him. They, in turn, are unaware that I am pursuing them. After all, Andrew needs us all.

⁺⁺ Bank Shot

Andrew

I have been called a lot of things in my thirteen years, but lazy or complacent has never been on the list. Crazy Jeal left me here, and I'm bored out of my mind. Despite having an all-access pass to his mini bar, if I don't break out of here soon, I will be certifiable. Black magic or no magic, I'm not even sure my captor is prepared for me when that time comes. I have scrolled through every single station on TV. I did manage to get caught up on all the latest episodes of *American Ninja Warrior,* and thank goodness for the premiere of "Shark Week." Otherwise, I might be banging my head against a wall.

I have no doubt that my crew is doing everything in their power to rescue me right now. My overactive imagination keeps jumping from thought to thought. It does keep me from feeling overwhelmed with despair. I'm confident that I will be all right, because we are a team. I feel myself getting teary eyed as a few memories with my brothers consume me. I recall the moments where we would race up the football ramps or them using me as a Halloween pawn, hoping to score more candy. I can almost taste the Bit-O-Honey in my mouth.

My tranquil thoughts evaporate after hearing some unusual sounds coming from outside the door. I highly doubt Lafitte knocks for anyone, and besides, the man should have his own key to this little dungeon. I position myself next to the handle while pressing my ear firmly against the door.

"Andrew? Andrew, are you inside?" It's a girl's voice, and I'm the only Andrew around. I can't pass up my opportunity for freedom.

"Yes!"

I hear loud footsteps accompanied by loud voices. I'm certain that one of the voices belongs to Lafitte. I would know that voice anywhere. The door opens, and I witness a peculiar sight. Riley is standing in front of me, which is definitely not a bad thing. Behind her is Lafitte. But there are more. The hallway is crowded with two uniformed men, and Booker and Shea are racing toward us. It has become a free-for-all, except for one thing. In the midst of all the chaos, Riley has removed herself and scooped me up. Still in character, Riley thanks all who are present for helping her save her little brother before dropping me back down to reality. Well, in this case, the carpeted hallway.

"He did it!" She points at Lafitte. Surprisingly, Lafitte appears more annoyed than anxious. In fact, the snide look on his face indicates that we may have played a good half, but the game isn't over.

Shea

Booker and I are about twenty feet behind Lafitte. I'm surprised he hasn't detected us following him. I imagine the only thing on his mind is having a romantic liaison with a girl who wants nothing to do with him. His pace is amazingly quick, especially for someone who hasn't worked out in almost two centuries.

We are about to enter a hidden hallway off the kitchen. Booker and I remain at the far end watching as Lafitte searches for a key. He fumbles around before he pulls the shiny object from his damp swimsuit. I believe the extra drink might be helping us already.

Maybe Booker and I are too cautious while hanging back the way we are, because the individual following us is much more brazen. The sight of Riley running right past us is mind boggling. She is flanked by two uniformed security officers. Where did all these people come from? Booker and I run after them. Naturally, our suntanned pirate is caught off guard. He jabs the key he has been fumbling with into Booker's face. That's it. I jump into the fray.

Here we are, a bunch of angry, sweaty people about to get into it in some secluded maze. I should be grateful to see the security guards. How am I ever going to explain this to my mom? There go the car keys. Luckily, the kitchen staff defend Booker's honor, and the heat seems to be on the pirate.

It doesn't really matter. I hear the reassuring sound of my little brother. Andrew is standing in the hallway clutching Riley's hand. (I'll talk to him about this aspect later.) I give Andrew the longest hug imaginable before Riley notices one important fact. Lafitte is gone.

⫶ Carry

Eva *(Final Night)*

There isn't much time left, and it all seems to be culminating tonight. Years in the making, a long-lost treasure and many who want to uncover it. Granted, not everyone involved is motivated by the same intentions. I don't know why all those particular events from so long ago have managed to go unearthed for so many years. I guess it is not my place to understand all the inner workings of this plot. I feel that I'm merely a vessel for the voices of the past.

My shop is dark and empty. I reach for a candle located on a dusty shelf hidden in a back room. Its formerly white exterior has become more of a taupe color, and the ancient wick is made of a rope-like material. I place it in the center of my discreetly tucked-away table. The table is covered with dust and is barely big enough for one person to sit at. No worries. I'm the only person here, and I don't plan on my experiment lasting too long. I close the curtains, making sure no additional light peeks inside the room. One last thing: I reach underneath my makeshift platform and find an object I rarely use.

I'm aware that many view crystal balls as beautiful windows into other dimensions, similar to the one in *Snow White*. I use my sphere only when absolutely necessary. The process is called scrying, and it scares me. Scrying has never come easily for me. I'm not like some of my family members, who have mastered this practice. I know some individuals who are even able to detect unearthly images simply by walking past dark puddles. I, on the other hand, use this art form only as a last resort. I believe this situation qualifies as now or never. Unlike so many others in my line of work, I choose to focus on seeing glimpses from the past, not the future. Most importantly, I don't want my mind to be filled with horrific images that I can't erase.

The fateful night was filled with many eyewitness accounts. Yet, for some strange reason, no one can remember any pertinent details. Then, of course, there is the realization that some priceless fortune seems to be floating around somewhere. The treasure should belong to no one, and yet should be claimed and honored by everyone. The sad truth is that should Lafitte locate the goods first, it will certainly be lost in his grasp. Always the ultimate cat burglar, the man will simply slip into obscurity for eternity, funded by a never-ending monetary supply. Quickly, I try to erase that possibility from my mind.

The dark sphere is much heavier than I remember it being and extremely cloudy. I blow out a couple of small puffs and place it next to the candle. I must do this. I sit on the chair while using an additional cushion for my backside. (This process might take a while.) The lights are off, and the only thing giving the room any type of sparkle is the sputtering candle flame. I rub my palms over the sphere as I try to erase all thoughts from my mind. I forget about the overflowing laundry bin in my utility room and the early start for tomorrow's basketball game. Instead, I focus on one night from a long time ago in a tiny coastal town. I try to imagine all the craziness and confusion and fear experienced by those living inside the chaos. After a couple of minutes, in which I struggle within myself, the flow of energy brings me back to a place that holds much more simplistic routines. I no longer see mothers waiting in car pool lines or kids with their backpacks strapped to their backs. Instead, I see mothers trying to protect their children and fathers praying their loyalties will still be rewarded when this evening ends.

The fog floats over to a place where a single building remains standing. The windows are covered with a thin veil of dew, and the wooden shutters are blowing back and forth, creating a synchronized clapping sound. The storm is particularly severe. I hear voices within. People are covering their faces to protect them from all the objects being blown around. I squeeze my eyes tighter, desperately hoping to gain entrance into the inner sanctum that is the study. Once there, I detect more people, and finally I see Lafitte. The man seems a bit worried, not in total control, as he most certainly is used to being. Thomas stands in the center of the room, completely quiet, watching those around him.

My head is pounding, but I refuse to break my connection. Again, I'm reminded of how brutal the scrying process can be and why I have never been a big fan of this activity. I grasp the edge of the table. My body is tense. I see Evelyne. She is gathering some of her belongings as Lafitte follows her around like a devoted lap dog. I catch a brief image of the three devoted slaves, including Booker and Caesar.

Finally, my sight is glued to the blankness of the room. The moment is now. It appears as if the cast of characters is all out for themselves. Thomas is curiously absent. Booker and Evelyne are conversing in a far corner of the room, and Jean is spying on them. Their respective plans appear to be officially in motion.

The rain keeps streaming down. The visibility outside is basically zero. I can already predict the outcome of some of the evening's events. First up, Thomas head toward one of the ships, thinking he has outsmarted his boss. The pirate follows his overly ambitious pro-tégée, stunned to learn that he has misplaced his trust.

My focus needs to remain on what is happening inside the study. I shake my head, trying to regain my concentration on the makeshift wooden building. They are there. Booker is holding a medium-sized satchel while scooting out the front door, unnoticed in the downpour. Evelyne remains inside her official sanctuary as she prepares to leave. I force myself to go back to Booker. I see him scooting alongside the building's exterior, looking up every so often. Sure enough, he is heading for the animals and the infamous trough. He takes one last look around before taking a huge leap of faith into the awaiting water.

The process begins. I see a cyclone caused by high winds, rain, and, of course, magic. The top of Booker's head (pre-flattop, and Ball hair days) is engulfed by the water. The athletic man is being sucked into a new unknown world. At that point, things become a bit more interesting.

Caesar decides to partake in the fun and follows his friend into the slobbery box of water. Every muscle in my body is tight, and I'm beginning to perspire. I feel as if I'm actually present in the moment, and my head snaps back, facing the ceiling. I can smell the rain and even feel the despair in everyone's thoughts. My body begins rocking side to side. I delve even deeper.

Then, out of nowhere, my connection is severed, and the lights turn on. I open my eyes, only to have a large hand, minus the attached arm, encased by a black leather glove cover my mouth. I'm no longer swaying but sitting upright. I'm officially scared! I force myself to see what or who snapped me out of my trance. There isn't an actual body. Instead, I simply see a hand with a finger waving in the air, as if to say, "No, no, no." Then the hand evaporates. I'd say tonight's scrying session has officially come to a close.

⁝ Zone

Shea

Booker texted, instructing us to meet up on the beach at our "spot." It appears we have all upgraded to secret spot status. He claims that Eva might have some insight for us. I sure hope so. It's our last night on the island, after all. Once again, a good night's rest is out of the question. The sad thing is that now it seems so normal to meet with a modern-day priestess.

We sit on the sand, forming a circle, and finally catch a glimpse of Eva strolling up. She wraps her fuzzy cardigan tightly around her waist before giving us a genuine smile. She appears to be in a pleasant mood. I choose to be optimistic.

Andrew is fidgeting nonstop, and Flynn is a nervous wreck. I think the rest of us are just too tired and exhausted to feel any fear about being here. Eva begins speaking before even reaching her destination. She gives us no time for pleasantries. "I was able to look into the past and see some of what actually happened. However, I couldn't see what happened to any treasure." Eva goes into detail with a recap of her vision. "The bottom line is that Caesar is the last person I saw in possession of the bag. It definitely wasn't Booker."

Booker looks at us while throwing up his arms. "Like I said, here is the real question: why hasn't Caesar just escaped with the loot if he had it?" We all ponder this mystery until Booker interrupts our thoughts. "You don't believe for a second that Ms. E. just let my man Caesar follow me to this space with full rights to that money, do ya? Caesar was no different than me. He just wanted a fresh start. Ms. Evelyne helped him out but with some extra instructions, that's all."

Eva hangs on every word before she takes over the conversation. "I couldn't see everything, but I agree with what Booker is implying. I'm almost certain she would never have allowed that bag to come over here with no strings attached. It's pretty obvious that she never intended for Lafitte to get his hands on it. She wanted everything to come over here on this side."

At that moment, we all come to the undeniable conclusion that these will be the only clues we receive. We must forget about the hows and whys and concentrate on what we have been given. We must uncover the treasure before Lafitte discovers it. Evidently, it all boils down to the old adages "finders, keepers" and "possession is nine-tenths of the law."

I look at Eva. "Do you have any special spell for us, any extra brain power?"

"This is all a matter of being true inside your hearts," Eva replies quietly. "Don't get me wrong; there is certainly magic in the air. We have all seen some of it by now. The thing is, loyalty can overcome it."

The distant sounds from far-away ships are the only thing distracting us. Riley places her head on my shoulder, and a tingling feeling goes down my spine. We're all deep in thought. Then Andrew jolts into an upright position. "I know where it is."

We turn to Andrew, trying to understand how he can be so certain. Despite Andrew's frequent carefree attitude, he exudes steely determination. I've only seen this side to him right before he takes a game-winning shot. "Everyone keeps bringing up Caesar. I believe this is important. I think he knows some things we don't. Our first night at the pier, dude gave me travel brochures and some cheesy gold coins. I didn't want the coins, except for the chocolate ones. So, I dropped the rest. I'm telling you, the guy was persistent. I believe the coins have something to do with all this."

With everything that we just heard, our crew is on the move again. Besides, what vacay is complete without one more visit to a closed theme park?

Matt

It is our final night here, and we will be spending it beneath the stars and moonlight. Did I mention that the idyllic setting is being undercut by the fact that we are sneaking into Pleasure Pier? After a quick phone call to my mom, alerting her to an impromptu "team meeting," we head out.

Upon arrival, we hide the bikes behind a few giant logs protruding from the sand. The stillness of the amusement park is unnerving, to put it mildly. Unlike our visit here a few nights ago, the only thing I hear is a constant buzzing noise coming from the vending machines. I'm certain of one thing: I will never look at Ferris wheels the same way again.

Andrew is our official leader. The rest of us use the flashlights on our phones to make our way through all the deserted paths, hoping not to twist an ankle. As we make a right turn in front of the "Walk the Plank" ride, we hear a loud cackle, which causes us to do the highest vertical jumps of our basketball careers. Great. We have definitely entered the designated pirate section. Standing in front of us is a life-sized figure of Captain Lafitte, complete with an eyepatch and a colorful parrot on one shoulder. The mechanical crook also speaks. "Ahoy, hand over all your loot." Geeze, these arcade designers haven't portrayed his image anywhere near the real deal. I wish the guy was only that scary. I suppose no one could have anticipated that the bearded goon, wearing the latest Tommy Bahama duds, is much more frightening.

After passing the final bin of toys and kiosks offering up the grandest cocktails on the seawall, we arrive at the "Treasure Hunt" game. I vaguely recall Andrew and Dax grabbing their souvenirs here, along with a treasure map. Andrew is getting increasingly excited as he positions us into a tight huddle. He grabs a crinkled piece of paper from his back pocket and tries to flatten it out. "See, there's a red star. It has to be here. Something is supposed to be here. It's in plain sight."

We begin making 360s, trying to decipher exactly where someone might have hidden a clue. Of course, the only thing that catches Flynn's eye is the leftover popcorn, which is still inside one of the machines. "When in Rome," he says before helping himself to a big carton of stale treats. I must admit that I, too, am starving. I'm not even going to pretend I'm immune to the lingering aroma of food. Flynn and I are probably not the most dedicated detectives out here tonight, but we are capable of offering much-needed moral support.

"Of course. Andrew is right. It's in plain sight," Shea remarks.

The tokens. If the assumption is correct, who would have done all this? The small replica chest contains many black velvet bags. All the pouches are adorned with the signature skull and crossbones on the front and are neatly packed with samples of doubloons. Some of the coins are gold, some silver, and some contain chocolates. I don't think any self-respecting kid could pass up the campy allure of buying tokens while standing on the same spot on which our dear friend stood back in the day. This must mean something! Booker reminds us that Caesar gave a particular bag to Andrew after basically stalking him all night.

"Let's dive in and see what we can find," Booker says. The task proves to be much more challenging than hitting rim for the first time. While those two decide to take the plunge, Flynn and I find another place to put our energy. Wouldn't you know it, there's a three-point shoot-out game! Flynn and I grab as many balls as our arms can hold. After all, we might as well get in some last-minute shooting practice while solving the world's problems.

"Okay, let's play 'Horse,'" I say. I suppose this is why none of us hear the incoming footsteps. Reality strikes back. One by one, we hush one another as we take cover behind the display posters. Light coming from some type of handheld device looms closer. As we lie in wait, a distinctive sound from a radio alerts us to approaching intruders. I'm only able to detect a shadow, but I hear an ongoing conversation debating whether or not there is any type of problem inside the park. After what seems like an eternity, the light finally moves away, and the voices become fainter.

We all take a few deep breaths and decide it is best to make our way back to the hotel. I think we have maybe taken just three small steps before something causes us to freeze in our tracks. "Whew." Booker glances back at us, reassuring us that the menacing noises belong simply to the plastic tarps that are supposed to be sealing off exhibits. Whatever. All any of this has done is remind me of every single horror movie I have ever watched. The plastic corners continue flapping, creating dark images in every corner we are forced to turn. I believe that, any minute now, Jason will leap out after me.

"Guys, can we pick up the pace?" Shea turns around and gives me a stern look while holding a finger to his lips. Suddenly, we all jump straight up.

"Ahoy!" In front of us is a movie screen, which has somehow turned itself on, accompanied by a glaring image of our pirate. This is all followed by a seriously twisted reminder. "Come back soon, if you dare." Shea shakes it off and tells us to keep going; it's only a promotional movie.

"Now what?" Flynn whispers to no one in particular.

As we all regain our sanity, Shea looks at Andrew. "Where's your bag of coins?" This question is pretty redundant. We know where the coins are.

Once we're safely back inside our room, we pull out every single token. One by one, we examine the worthless currency before Matt decides to pull out his glasses for an even closer look.

"What is it?" Booker asks.

"I don't know, but there are some seriously weird numbers on this one. It's kind of worn, but the other coins only have designs on them."

Grabbing the dull souvenir out of Matt's hand, Booker inspects it closely. "Of course! These aren't just random numbers. The digits represent an exact location."

I maneuver myself a little closer to Shea, trying to get a better look. None of this so-called money looks anything like my loose change. Booker briefs us on how things were located back in the days before Siri. The well-worn coins had two precise numbers. Shea is already on it and is hurriedly pulling up the mystery location. The rest of us sit patiently, except for Booker, who begins his usual pacing. I'm still astounded by his endless energy. Finally, he stops and faces us. "Think about it. Caesar took the bag. Either he has been the token guardian all these years, or someone else received it on this end. Homeboy might have been sneaky, but he never laid his hands on it. For whatever reason, he wanted to make sure Andrew had his hands on one particular coin. It got things going."

Just then, Shea looks up from his phone. "It's the gym."

⁝ Post Up

Eva *(Final Morning)*

It's been a long night, and having to get up early for the tournament meant no sleep for me. My head is bordering on a full-blown migraine, but I'm determined to make my little guy his favorite good luck breakfast. Just like clockwork, in he strolls, all suited up with his phone glued to his ear. God really did bless me when I became a mother. Deep down, I know I'm gifted with some unusual magic, most of which I keep hidden. However, nothing compares to the joy I get from seeing my baby smile. "Eat up. You're going to need fuel for those legs of yours." I proceed to pile his plate high with eggs, bacon, and plenty of carb-filled pancakes.

I hear the front door open and peek around to see who just walked in, expecting to find one of his teammates. Instead, I see Booker standing in my living room, wearing his trademark smile and holding a pair of crazy-looking kneepads. He gives me a huge embrace while tossing his gift on my counter. "Wear these, Daniel, for luck, man. Don't say I never gave you anything."

Daniel reaches for the offering and thanks Booker with a fist bump. "Dude, they're cool." The boy smiles (all six feet two inches of him) and then heads out to his waiting ride before reminding me not to be late. I assure him that I will make it in time for tip-off and see him out. Now to deal with Booker.

"Booker, if there is one thing I'm certain of, it's that Evelyne would never have sent that treasure over here without some strings attached. Caesar was simply the messenger. Spells and magic only last for so long before greater forces take over. It's a simple matter of elements, powers. I'm betting this secret has finally run its course."

While I was growing up, stories of Evelyne were mystical, even legendary. Hidden in my mother's boudoir was a sketch of the woman. The myth surrounding her was that her magic was untouchable. Many people were frightened by her, but some just wanted to use her. I imagine Lafitte fit into the latter category. However, the one thing I never heard regarding my enigma of a relative was that she was crooked. "I just can't imagine that she would have intended for Lafitte to possess the fortune. She wants you to find it before he does."

Booker and I sit silently for several minutes before he gets up. The sun is shining, and the day is officially beginning. Booker gives me a big embrace before going out the front door. "I don't suppose you have a fun spell to help my nerves, do ya?"

Shaking my head, I remind him that he has all the tools he needs. Well, I'm doing my best to keep things legal.

Matt

I must concentrate. Despite everything that has gone down during the last few hours, I will compartmentalize, block it out. I'm here to win a tournament. As I gather my gear, I locate my favorite shoes. Loosening the laces, I adjust the shoes to fit my feet. I prefer my footwear to fit snugly, and I like my socks to be pulled up to just the right spot on my calf. As I slip my right foot inside the low court shoes, the pressure encircling my ankle increases. What on earth? The force intensifies to such a degree that I feel a slight pain. Immediately, I reach down and grab my ankle, rotating it side to side. It is about then that I lose my patience. "Shea!"

A moment later, the bathroom door swings open, and Shea's concerned face appears. I suppose that after everything that has happened, I could have just whispered his name, and he would have come running. Before he can speak, I point down to my feet, which seem to be super-glued firmly to the floor. "Why am I stuck here?" Shea dutifully grabs my trusty Nike Kyries and pulls with all his might. We grunt and groan and produce some serious sweat.

"This is ridiculous! It's like there's some crazy spell on you!" Shea shouts.

It doesn't take much more of the current shenanigans before we both lose it. How much can teenagers be expected to take? My hopes of participating in the final game slowly evaporate into a bad dream. Yes, it's true that I have met some strange souls this past week. However, I can't even begin to guess who might be sufficiently irritated with me to want to pull off this sick joke.

After a few more fruitless minutes of push and pull, I decide to simply slip my feet out of the shoes. Ahhh! I feel the immediate comfort of the shaggy carpet beneath my socks. As Shea and I turn to face one another, giggles echo inside our room. One thing is certain: this warped sense of humor is definitely not coming from either of us. The chorus of giggling erupts into full-blown laughter and the shoes in question rise into the air. Up and up my new shoes go, high above our heads.

Of course. The air blossoms into a sweet aroma of magnolias and is soon joined by a slight mist, which begins filling our room. The expectant fog morphs into the shapely figure of a young lady, complete with a floating gown and long blown-out hair. Simone floats before us, her arms extended in greeting. She holds my shoes high with her half-visible hands. Sorry, but I'm not amused. Unfortunately, I fail to remember the ol' adage, "Think before you speak," as I lose my temper. "How dare you? I'm so done!"

One never quite knows how a ghost will react to being scolded. As soon as the words escape my lips, I regret it, and I even feel a sudden twinge of fear. Well, fear not, because Simone chooses to go the emotional route. I had no idea that ghosts shed tears. Her high cheekbones freeze up, and small droplets begin to flow. Immediately, Shea and I go into survival mode as we try reversing the damage.

"Simone, don't cry. It's just that I'm in a hurry and got extremely frustrated. Please! I'm sorry, okay?" Simone stares at us, and the water works get stronger. At this rate, we'll need to call maintenance, because puddles are forming on the carpet.

Shea reaches for her hand, but instead of reciprocating his token of affection, her sad image coils up like a small grass snake. Here we are, standing in our hotel room with drenched carpets trying to aid a ghost girl. What next? Why do I even ask? Simone decides to torpedo her spirit straight down inside my shoe. Her crying intensifies. Are you kidding me?

I notice Shea frantically texting someone. How I hope he is going to resolve our current drama. I guess it doesn't matter how many centuries have passed; feelings are still being hurt.

After a couple of knocks at the door, Thomas strolls in. "Hey, sight for sore eyes. I'm just going to give you two some much needed privacy," I blurt. Shea simply hands our favorite musketeer the shoe and walks to the other side of the room. Neither one of us can hear the conversation, but just watching some guy talking back and forth to a size-twelve shoe is rather unforgettable. Every once in a while, I detect Thomas having to speak with the opposite side of his mouth. Let's just say I think my past endeavors on the court have left a lasting aroma.

Thomas sets the footwear down and heads over to speak with us. In the background, Simone's dress reappears, and her distinctive floral smell grows even stronger. Thomas glances back at his betrothed, smitten as can be. "She wants you both to know that the treasure is somehow tied up with this final."

Well then, let's go.

As we approach the gym, my thoughts shift to my shot and getting loose. We park the car, and I reach for my bag. I push open my door and feel the hot early afternoon sun. My first instinct is to shut my eyes.

As my feet hit the scorching pavement, I hear the loudest rendition of Russ's "What they Want" I could ever imagine. In fact, I believe the ground might be shaking. As the music grows louder, the car in question turns around in the parking lot. It isn't just any car but a low-riding Nova, circa 1970. The vehicle comes to a stop, straddling two parking places, and the doors fly wide open. Honestly, I never knew a sedan could hold so many people. One by one, more and more people pour out onto the pavement. What on earth?

Out of curiosity, I take a few steps toward the pale yellow vehicle. I spot a fuzzy wheel cover and a few items dangling from the rear-view mirror. Finally, the driver's door swings open, unveiling Caesar. "Wus up, man?" He smiles, and I wave. No one can ever say these old-timers don't have huge personalities.

Once inside the gym, I hit the boards, and my determination comes rushing back. The drills run smoothly, and I feel confident. Maybe a little bit too confident. Every so often, I find myself glancing over to the far side of the court and catch a glimpse of the competition. Often, this little dance evolves into head games. Luckily, we've all been playing together for a while. Basketball is a team sport; that much we feel. It doesn't matter if someone makes a mistake, because in the end, it's a group win or a group loss. I see the clock ticking down rapidly to game time, and the shooter shirts are thrown over to the sideline. Just like magic, last night seems to evaporate. The focus is on the here and now. How much do we love this game? I shove my mouthpiece in and am ready to go.

⁞ One on One

Shea

Word of mouth was that we would make it to the championship, and we have done just that. Despite what that sounds like, it was no easy task. However, here we are, about to face Booker's Galveston locals for the grand prize. I didn't even think to ask Booker who he was going to back today; doesn't really matter. This has been a hard-fought tournament, and only two teams are left standing. This past week has been filled with nonstop action, frightening occurrences, and many lifelong memories. (No one would believe any of this if we ever decided to spill.) Still, it would be a nice conclusion if we actually pulled off this win before heading back to reality. The only clue any of us have to go on at this point is that we needed to make it here on this particular afternoon. Here we are. I must say, I see no treasure. As of right now, I'm officially checked out. I'm benching myself from all thoughts of Jean Lafitte. We are in it to win it.

I'm still warming up, trying some last-minute plays that I probably should have memorized by now. In the corner of my eye, I see Booker arrive. He seems rather cautious, pausing for a few seconds before taking a seat right in the middle of the stands. I notice parents filing in, careful to sit directly behind their respective teams. You must respect the loyalty in all this. I'm sure by now that everyone is worn out and emotionally exhausted. However, no one would let on that their thoughts are slowly drifting to the errands they must complete by noon on Monday. No matter; if these spectators only knew what else might be at stake during this next hour, a technical will seem insignificant.

I release one more shot before noticing Eva stroll into the gym. Unlike Booker, she never breaks her stride and continues climbing into the bleachers to find a seat. Alas, she sits directly to Booker's right, which allows her to be behind the home team. True to form, Booker remains Switzerland. The game should be underway within mere minutes, and the stands are packed.

Other than my mom, the person I'm mostly concerned about being here is Riley. Sure enough, she and her group finally arrive. I'm sorry, but the girl is hot! I know that every guy thinks his current crush is the end all, but Riley really is. She and her pack make their way to the far end of the gym, firmly establishing their place in my team's camp. Riley's long hair is loose, and she resonates the most golden glow imaginable. Honestly, I believe her legs might need a couple of yardsticks to accurately measure their length. She has thrown on a simple pair of boyfriend cut-offs and has topped them off with a chic looking hi-lo T. I'm officially whipped.

It's time. The arena is so jam packed that even the maintenance workers are jockeying for position to catch a good view of the final show. I suppose I should count myself lucky, because at least I have a courtside seat. I grab the back of my shoes one more time, hoping to give them one final wiping off. I feel prepared, but then I detect all the energy shift. I practically gulp for a bit of air before noticing him.

He is here. Jeal has arrived. I should have known he wasn't going to miss an epic finale. The man cruises inside without a care in the world. Typical. This man is the most pompous individual I have ever known. God help me if I ever have to study him in class or, worse, write an essay about him. He's totally overrated.

The obnoxious noises blaring over the loudspeakers indicate the game is about to begin. Both teams huddle on their respective sides for one last minute with their coaches. I'm absorbed in the pep talk before instinctively cupping my ears due to loud buzzing noises. I look around and notice that players and fans alike are bracing themselves for something insanely disturbing. I see the officials racing over to barricade the exterior doors, which have blown wide open. The force of the winds cause us all to fall to our knees. The buzzing sounds increase to the level of an old-fashioned steam engine heading toward us. Despite everyone trying to regain control of this absurd situation, the doors fly off their hinges! Strange doesn't even begin to explain this!

The heavy winds won't cease, but they are only part of the problem. The incoming buzzing sounds are the result of thousands of butterflies invading the sports complex. Everyone ducks and tucks their head between their knees. Now, I realize butterflies are relatively harmless, but imagine thousands fluttering around at once. It's not fun.

After about thirty minutes, and the help of some industrial-sized fans, the pesky critters redirect their flight pattern to a different location. We all do our best to act as if none of this has fazed us in the least. As management dusts off the floor, people readjust their clothes.

"Don't you know that butterflies are the symbol of resurrection?" Flynn says.

Thomas

I admit I have never actually been to a basketball tournament or, for that matter, any sporting event. I have managed to figure out that each team must place a large round ball into an elevated hoop belonging to the opposite team. There is definitely a lot of aggression, as each team tries maneuvering the ball down the court to the other side. Every so often, the people with the horrid striped shirts blow their whistles, which stops play altogether. The people watching all this, as I am, are getting rather boisterous. "Scoreboard check!" one fan yells to another. I'm confused. Are we all to take note of the official tally? I'm not sure. It does seem a shame that Simone can't join me on this journey. Maybe this type of task is something that she and I should work on in the future. Truth be told, I don't really know Daniel. I'm rooting for Shea and the clan. At this point, we all share some real history. Come to think of it, my experiences are like those of modern-day frat brothers, minus the kegs.

The game is extremely fast-paced and even a bit of fun. However, the mere presence of Jean leaves me a bit out of sorts. There he sits, directly across from me, pretending to watch the game. Unless I've been stuck in a time warp for even longer than I have, there is no way that he comprehends what he is watching on this court any more than I do. Unlike me, he shows up wearing his bandwagon Spurs jersey. Nice touch. Jean is only here, because he's been trailing us and hopes he can outmaneuver us. Whatever is really going on, it's all been boiling down to this day, this game. So many years have swept by, and so many stories have been told, but the presence of this particular group of young men has triggered some type of conclusion to a long-drawn-out mystery. In many ways, this tale is much more than an unsolved mystery. It is also closure for two heartbroken lovers and for two worlds needing to be permanently severed. Boy, life sure can be complicated.

I try to think about the match. It's becoming too tense for me. The numbers on the shiny scoreboard change constantly. One second, one team is ahead, and the next second, the other team inches up. I'm convinced that the miracle drug, Prozac, is prescribed for these types of scenarios. Spare us all!

The clock drops to the final minute. People are standing, and the decibel level inside the building is at an all-time high. The game is tied. I detect that strategy is now playing a crucial role in this final act of today's closing curtain. Daniel has the ball. He moves, takes a shot, and somehow the ball continues circling inside the rim. The ball completes at least ten circles before finally dropping through the net. The crowd erupts. Everyone around me prepares for the game's final drive. (Of course, this little song and dance seems to last forever, what with all the deliberate fouls and time outs.) Thirty seconds remain on the clock, and Galveston's full-court press can't prevent Shea from getting the ball back down the court. The time is now. What is everyone really made of? (If the hotel concierge thing doesn't pan out for me, maybe I should consider going into sports broadcasting.)

With ten seconds remaining, all eyes are glued on Shea. He darts in and out, drives, stops, and pulls up to take the final shot of the game. Once again, the ball seems to go in slow motion. The perfectly shot ball flies through the air with a mastered arc, heading directly toward the goal. Maybe time really can stand still. The ball goes around and around the inside of the rim, just as it did moments earlier in the other goal. I prepare myself for the overtime that is sure to follow. Then, as if an invisible hand is pushing from beneath, the ball falls *outside* the net, and the final buzzer blares.

Game over. The Galveston Pirates have pulled it off. I remain standing in total disbelief. I finally manage to look over at Shea. I see him mouthing something to Booker in the stands. "Magic?"

Booker laughs. "No, you choked," he mouths back. They both laugh.

‡ Backboard

Shea

The medals are being handed out, and the picture taking has begun. I suppose if we had to lose to anyone in the championship game, I would have chosen Daniel's team. I'd like to chalk it up to sleep deprivation, but the Pirates are a pretty strong group. How ironic that the locals decided on that particular moniker for their team.

As I line up behind Flynn, I see Booker and Eva in the crowd. Jeal is watching everyone, as well. Is he aware that the player's jersey he is wearing has been traded twice? The good thing is, the man seems as clueless as the rest of us are right now when it comes to understanding any of this.

I prep myself for the realization that none of us may ever know what went down this past week, but then my train of thought is broken by the inevitable trophy presentation. Both teams make their way to center court wearing the medals around their necks. I have overheard that the final ceremonial act will be accompanied with a huge surprise. I hope that means great internet on the drive home. The focal point shifts toward a tall man carrying an even taller piece of hardware. The grandness of it all is followed by simultaneous flashes that blind us. The applause gets louder as the larger-than-life individual walks down the line, shaking our hands.

No way! It's Shaquille O'Neal! Shaq! Honestly, I can't believe my eyes! All visions I might have just had of shots I should have made or long-lost fortunes are eclipsed by meeting one of the NBA's all-time greats. My hands are already shaking before the great man himself appears in front of me. His hands are enormous, and he reaches for my sweaty palms. Somehow, I muster up enough courage to look him in the eyes. "Congrats, man. You'll get em' next time," he says to me. Is it just my imagination, or did the superstar athlete, whose image has graced cereal boxes and whose face has covered many walls, just give me a knowing wink?

After greeting every player, Shaq takes his position front and center for the trophy presentation. He hands the two-ton award to the locals, and the crowd goes wild. (Okay, maybe the trophy doesn't really weigh two tons, but it does appear to be extremely heavy.) With the coach's assistance, the trophy is raised high over the heads of the new champs, and the cheers grow even louder.

Despite losing, our crew joins in the celebration. The overhead speakers blare music, and some people bust out some serious dance moves. I notice Riley smiling at me, and I can't help but feel that this moment is meant to be. Maybe this is similar to the feeling that revelers experience during Mardi Gras, but for a select few of us, the all-consuming emotions overcoming us are at an all-time high. This must be what it's like when you read the final page of a mystery novel without reading the inside chapters.

As we look at the masterpiece that is the final award, it begins to glow. Its intensity beams so bright it appears to have an extra light shining down on it from above. The thing is, none of this intensity is being caused by extra strobe lights, and there sure isn't any confetti being strewn atop it. No, the brightness is coming from its own energy source and it is most definitely not from this world. Am I the only person who can see it? Evidently not, because I notice that Booker, Eva, Matt, Andrew, and even Jeal are transfixed by the shininess of the trophy. Time stands still.

We just found our treasure.

Well, that's it then. It must have been Evelyne's plan all along to see to it that when the day came for Jeal to finally make his way over to the modern world, he wouldn't be able to get his hands on the fortune. I may never understand why any of us had to be involved, but we did. One thing is for sure: I will never forget this trip.

Back at the hotel, I throw bags, blankets, and stinky clothes into waiting cars in the parking lot. I no longer care who owns what. I glance up and notice Booker strolling toward me. Good guy that he is, he arrives with the crazy dog on a leash just in time for Andrew to take him home. I overhear Andrew trying to explain to my mom how we managed to acquire a new pet. I believe this might be a long drive home. I doubt Flynn's donkey will be making the two-hundred-mile trip.

How is it possible to feel such a sudden overwhelming sadness at leaving some dude who I met less than a week ago? As Booker hugs each of us and we exchange social media addresses, he stops in front of me. "It's been real, man. I'm gonna keep on your radar."

I can't help but smile before giving the old soul a huge embrace. I might have shed tears, had it not been for Riley approaching. My gosh, how much more can a guy take?

"Shea," she says. Her big, brown eyes pierce right through me, and I can't even find the words. Luckily, words aren't necessary, as Riley leans in for a kiss. I'm not sure what startles me more, her self-assuredness or the fact that our kiss occurs in front of all those closest to me. What I'm sure of is that it was quite a kiss. Suddenly, Riley turns shy, and her cheeks change from suntanned to several shades of deep red. She looks down at the ground, hoping to avoid everyone's reactions. Ever so slowly, I tilt her face up toward mine. All I can do is smile while giving her a reassuring hug.

"Snapchat," I say.

Always one for his comic relief timing, Andrew appears, right on cue. Grabbing my arm, he spins me around, determined to include us in his FaceTime call with Thomas. The image before us is Thomas beaming as he wears a perfectly pressed Galvez uniform. It seems only fitting that he should be a Galveston tour guide for the oldest hotel on the island. I can't think of anyone more qualified to offer some insight into the area's best pirate and ghost tours.

As we continue saying our goodbyes, the image of a blurry figure floats right through our friend. Never one to be left out of anything, Simone's white gown appears to be floating in front of her much more solid fiancé. I'm sure that if we were with them, we would smell one last whiff of her distinctive magnolia scent.

"I've figured out the phone thing. I will stay in touch," Thomas assures us. Theirs will be a wedding I definitely won't want to miss.

Booker approaches us for his final round of goodbyes. I have to ask him one more question. "What happened to Jeal?"

The free man shrugs. "He's here, and he's not leaving. Heck, this is a brand-new world for him. I wouldn't worry too much though. The dude is gonna have to find something else to do."

With that, we all go our separate ways.

⁝ Flop

End Game (Shaq)

When I first cast this spell, I had no idea that it would all wind down to some good action on the court. I remember it as if it was yesterday, wanting to make sure the goods were kept safe. I knew I couldn't take them over on my back and that Booker shouldn't be burdened with a century of responsibility. Booker and Caesar did the grunt work for me, and I just picked up the pieces, so to speak. There was so much craziness that night that even the Galvez kitchen staff didn't know what was going on. It was simple, really. I was just the last soul to arrive in the new dimension. The bag was still lying there right by the fresh produce. I scooped it up and finalized the instructions. No one will tamper with the fortunes of the people for at least 150 years. Even I have my limits. Sure, it has changed its form over time, but it always remains in full public view. It's a shame that people don't pay more attention to their surroundings as they go about their day-to-day life. I, on the other hand, have given myself ample opportunities to fully experience this new age. I did find baseball a bit boring. Politics was so frustrating! I must say I have thoroughly enjoyed the sports world, and being Shaquille O'Neal is quite fun. The commercial endorsements have paid extremely well.

These past few days have been confusing and crazy, with all the questions floating around about the stolen treasure. The treasure will continually remain with the people now that it was "found" by sincere souls. The good news is that Thomas and Simone have been reunited. I won't even begin to hurt my head thinking about the many obstacles they might soon face. Bonds between brothers have been strengthened, and new friendships have been formed, despite how unworldly they might be.

The final ceremony has ended, and parents are heading out the door. Most of these people have no idea that today was so much more than simply enjoying some great competition. I'm beat! My work here is done. I need to shake off this middle-aged fan. Is he even slightly aware that he and I go way back? I doubt it. He thinks I'm a retired superstar and that his wit and charm will seduce me the way it has countless others. It never did and never will. However, I will continue playing the game.

Jean Lafitte appears eager to shake my hand. Seriously? Can he change his jersey first? I mean, the least he can do is wear a Lakers or Magic shirt. His actions are dubious at best. Obviously, he has no idea that I can read his thoughts. He has become way too clingy for my taste. "One last pic, man. It's time to put this pretty thing to rest."

I continue speaking to him while I make my way over to the infamous trophy case. It will be foolproof. The good news for all those amateur treasure hunters out there is that I've left some scattered memorabilia all along these waterways. I like maintaining the legend.

Jean wants a selfie, and he shoves a selfie stick in my face. He continues making fake conversation, but I have had enough. He is still talking as I gently, maybe a bit forcefully, show him the door. Finally,

I'm alone. I move aside a few pre-existing awards and place the trophy front and center. It is protected. It belongs to the people and was won fair and square.

After admiring my hard work, I decide it is time to make my exit out the back door. It isn't easy ducking my seven-foot-one-inch frame down a little to clear the doorway. This has been a long time coming. With one last look around, I place the key behind my ear and contemplate a good place to eat. I'm always hungry. You should have seen my appetite when I was still playing. It was scary.

As I push the door open, I feel a rush of hot air hit my face. Not a soul is around, past or present. No one witnesses my legs gradually get shorter, my large feet diminish from size twenty-two to a demure women's size seven, or my workout clothes transforming into a long pleated skirt. My name is Evelyne, and I must figure out a new person to live through for a while. Decisions are always tough. After all, there are so many intriguing characters out there at the moment. Beyoncé would be fun. Bill Gates would be challenging. However, I sure have enjoyed watching *The Voice*, and Blake Shelton seems to know how to live. I've always wanted to sing.

My work here is done.

‡ Free Throw

Shea *(Six Months Later)*

I doubt too many days have passed where I haven't thought about last summer, at least once. We've all kept in touch. Booker and Thomas weren't technically on the team, but they are now family. We are most definitely family.

In the meantime, I've packed for our holiday cruise, which will last an entire week. Wouldn't you know it, the ship departs from Galveston. As usual, Andrew is gearing up for some one-on-one on the ship, but our first order of business is the mandatory meeting. We are in our designated spots on deck awaiting our safety instructions. It is taking everything Andrew has in him to remain still. I decide it's the perfect opportunity to take an impromptu pic on board. Riley will certainly get a kick out of this. A few light-hearted shoves later, the official captain's welcome fills the ocean air.

"Hello, and welcome aboard. Please let me assure you that the crew and I are determined to make this journey a trip of a lifetime."

There is much more to his speech, but I don't hear it. I glance toward the far end of the ship, and I swear I see the tail end of a Cartagena flag waving in the wind. Is that violin music? It appears Jeal has found himself a new job.

CPSIA information can be obtained
at www.ICGtesting.com
Printed in the USA
FFHW022012300119
50371113-55483FF